SAVING THROW

Table Topped #3

Alex Silver

CONTENTS

Copyright

This is a work of fiction. Names, characters, places, and incidents either are the product of the author's imagination or are used fictitiously. Any resemblance to actual persons, living or dead, events, or locales is entirely coincidental. All registered trademarks are the property of their owners.

ISBN (print): 978-1-7773563-7-8
ISBN (ebook): 978-1-7773563-8-5

BLURB

Rene was my first everything. Best friend, first kiss, first love, first heartbreak.

Seven years after walking out of my life, they tear open old wounds with a single photo of a smiling little boy and the message they're coming home.

Mo has my smile and Rene's eyes. It kills me that I didn't know about him sooner. As furious as the news Rene kept such a major secret makes me, I want a relationship with my son more than I want to rehash old arguments. Besides, Rene has more baggage than the 747 they flew in on, and I swore off love the first time they left me heartbroken.

When I learn Rene and Mo need a place to stay while they settle into life in Vancouver, it sounds like a perfect opportunity. I've got a spare room. What better way to figure out co-parenting than living together? It's not like I'm going to fall for the ex who hurt me deeper than anyone else could. That would be ridiculous.

Saving Throw is the third M/NB romance in the Table Topped series. It features Errol, demisexual panromantic production coordinator who likes to be in control and his first love, Rene, a non-binary trans masc ex-hockey player turned coach.

CW: Past mentions of a physically abusive alcoholic parent and portrayals of trauma/PTSD related to that, secret teenage pregnancy and related gender dysphoria/difficulty with accessing medical care. Side characters struggle with infertility.

CHAPTER 1

Errol

The last person I expect a message from on my art commission page is Rene Dumond. Pronounced Ree-nee, no matter how anyone else says it should sound or be spelled, they're particular about that. The last time I saw Rene in person was at their high school graduation party. Where they very publicly broke my heart, then stomped on the pieces, threw every piece into a fire and laughed about it. I might be the slightest bit bitter about how things ended.

We didn't keep in touch when they moved to Montreal. I was already in my second year at UBC, the University of British Columbia, in Vancouver, being a year older. Rene got almost a full ride to play hockey for McGill. An undisclosed injury forced them to ride the bench during their first year. They went on to play for the Montreal Canadienne's for a year after school before hanging up their skates. Not that I followed my ex's career. Or recall verbatim what Rene had to say about the deplorable inequity between the women's hockey league and men's hockey. The women's league didn't even pay their players until a couple years ago. Even that is a pittance.

Ugh. Rene ruined my perfect indifference toward sportsball of every kind. I'm the only one of my friends who watches any sporting events. Pia's the only person who knows why. And only because they caught me drunk and melancholy one day at uni, when Rene's team was on television.

I haven't heard anything about Rene since they retired at the end of their first pro season. They could be anywhere, doing anything they please. And somehow, that includes sending me a commission request. To draw a charcoal portrait from a digital photo of a gap-toothed kid.

The kid in the picture could be Rene's twin. They have the same dimple when they smile.

I don't think I can handle drawing my ex's son. I'm not great at guessing kids' ages, but they must have had him not long after leaving home for him to appear school-aged. Not long after we ended. My heart squeezes in my chest as I read the message attached to the commission request.

Errol,

Surprise! Hey stud, didn't think I'd find you so easy. Who knew you'd really make something of your art? Well, you always said you would. Hope it pays better than hockey paid me.

So. You might be wondering why now? There's no easy way to say this, hope you're sitting down. I've thought about how I'd tell you every day for the past seven years. Hoo, boy. Here goes. You know how I ran off to Quebec early for school? Yeah, there was a reason for that. His name is Monet. Figured I'd give him a piece of his dad. You liked Monet's art, right?

Please don't be mad. I hadn't decided if I was keeping him, and I didn't want to tell you only to decide I couldn't handle a pregnancy. Then it seemed too late, and I didn't want to screw up your life. Make you choose between school and us. So I let you go. And ensured you wouldn't chase after me or pine or whatever. I didn't mean the things I said that day.

I'm sorry. I should have told you sooner. He knows who you are. I never kept that from him. Shit. I'm going to hit send before I chicken out again. Hate me, not Mo, okay?

TL;DR: Surprise, you're a dad! His name is Mo, and he's 6. Photo attached. Please don't hold my being a teenage dumbass when I had him against him.

Yours,

Rene

I don't have any words for the impotent rage that brief note inspires in me. This is typical Rene. Impulsive. Rene always acted without thinking things through or considering how it would affect others. It made them fun to be around when we were kids.

Rene always had the best ideas to make our own fun in our small town. And I was always the one stuck getting us back out of whatever trouble their brilliant ideas got us into. From a joyride in my dad's car before we had our licenses, to painting a giant pride flag across the high-school football field's midline right before homecoming. Rene always walked away smelling like roses, and I always bore the brunt of their recklessness. Well, sort of. If Rene's dad had found out about half the shit we pulled, they'd have paid a much steeper price than I ever did. Hence why I always claimed sole credit for our antics.

And now Rene says I have a kid I never knew existed. A

kid who has my dark hair and lanky limbs. And of course they saddled the kid with a name like Monet. Mo suits the boy in the picture, with his impish grin. A wave of longing hits me then. Grief for all the time I've already missed out on having with this kid who is a piece of me. All the long sleepless nights that I haven't been there for Mo or Rene. Innumerable firsts I'll never get back. I'll be a stranger to him.

My first impulse is to reply with an angry screed about how Rene had no right to hide the pregnancy. To keep my son from me. But I can't deny that it had been Rene's choice. From watching Pia struggle with carrying Rain, I can imagine how hard that must have been for them. How much harder was it, all alone and in a strange city? If they had told me, I would have gone with them to Montreal. My life would be completely different.

Well, it's getting upended now. I can't undo the past seven years, but there is no power on earth that will make me miss out on the rest of Mo's life. Rene included their phone number at the bottom of the message. I punch it into my phone, then think better of calling. I'm too angry to sound calm.

Errol: Hey, Rene. This is Errol. I got your commission request. This isn't some sick joke, is it? I am so mad at you for keeping this from me. I don't even have words for it. But I'll get over that. I want to meet him. Tell me when and where.

Rene: Do you hate me?

Errol: Never. Furious at you, but I could never hate you.

Rene: We're moving back to BC. Mo and me. I got a job.

Assistant coaching for a junior league team. He wants to meet you, too.

Errol: Have you arranged housing?

Rene: Working on finding something affordable. Not a ton of options. Looking up listings for short-term rentals until we find something I can afford.

Errol: Where is the job?

Rene: Burnaby. With the Greatridge Oilers.

Errol: I'm still living in Burnaby. Move in with me? At least until you find something better. I want to know my kid.

Rene: Do you have enough room?

Errol: I've got a futon in my home office, and I can get an extra cot for Mo.

Rene: That works. If it won't be an imposition? He's so much like you it hurts. You're going to love him.

Errol: You're family, no imposition. So he's a total geek? Has he seen the new Star Trek?

Rene: He asks for it almost as much as you made me watch TNG ;)

Errol: Definitely my kid.

Rene: I wasn't with anyone else.

Errol: Never meant to imply you were.

Rene: It's nice talking to you again. Like old times.

Errol: There's no going back to old times, Rene. You

broke my heart when you left. I never suspected you could tear it out all over again years later and crush it more.

Heck, I hadn't realized I had that much heart left to crush, after Rene left. There's a long pause before the next message appears.

Rene: I'm sorry.

Errol: I don't want you to be sorry. I just want to know Mo. And seriously, why would you name him Monet?

Rene: He's spent most of his life in Quebec, it's a nice French name. And I told you, I wanted to give him whatever pieces of you I could.

Errol: I wish I'd been there.

Rene: Me too. We've still got a ton of packing to get through so I can ship or get rid of everything that won't fit in our suitcases by Saturday. I can send you the flight details if you want to meet us at the airport this weekend?

Errol: I'll be there.

Typical Rene, leaving things to the last minute. I've got a day and a half to prepare. It'll be a scramble to get the office turned into a guest room, but it's doable. Bright side, this way I won't have time to obsess over whether the kid will resent me and everything that could go wrong with Rene and my reunion.

CHAPTER 2

0 2

Rene

Monet sobs about leaving our shabby apartment. I shouldn't have told him to say goodbye. That we're never coming back to the only home he's ever known. This will be good. I've told us both over and over that we're doing the right thing. Mo's starting grade one this year. My little November baby will be almost seven, among the oldest in his class. That's okay. It's good. Everything is wonderful.

Mo's the only reason I'm not chewing my nails down to the cuticles right now. I can't show him how nervous I am. We're going to see Errol today. He's meeting his other dad for the first time and I have to show him it's okay, there's nothing to fear about the flight or what comes after.

"Papa?" Mo asks. He kicks the back of my seat with his light up sneakers. They flash annoyingly in my periphery, bright against the predawn darkness of the rental car's interior.

"Yeah, Momo?" I glance back at him in the rearview. He's getting so tall. Like Errol. How many millions of times have I looked at him and seen the one who got away in his features? I have zero right to get upset over the results of my decisions. It was my choice to walk away from my life and hide Monet. I can't undo the hurt I caused Mo and Errol by doing that. Feeling some small measure of it is the least I deserve for being an impulsive idiot.

"*Quand nous arrivons,* we're going to meet Daddy?"

"Yeah, kiddo. Daddy said he'd be waiting for us when we get there. And um, people don't speak as much French there," I remind him, biting my lip. It will be a change, but kids adapt. That's what my folks always said after every move. You'll make new friends. Kids are resilient. It was BS then, and it's probably BS now, but the die is cast and I'm bringing Mo home.

"*Pourquoi donc*?" Monet whines.

"Because kiddo. It'll be okay."

"Because why?" he demands, as if I'll have a better answer if he asks in English.

"Momo, why don't you nap until we get to the airport, Papa's driving," I say, trying not to let on that I'm second guessing everything.

"*Pas fait dodo.* Not tired." Mo kicks my seat harder in emphasis and I grit my teeth against snapping back at him to just stop and let me focus on the road.

At least the highway traffic is sparse at four in the morning as we drive to the airport. I pull into the rental place with the car. Then it's a mad dash to wrestle Monet loose, grab our bags, pile his booster seat on top and somehow get him and our stuff to the terminal shuttle bus. I feel bedraggled as the courtesy shuttle driver gives me a sympathetic look and the other passengers scowl at having to wait for us to take a seat.

Monet pokes my face to get my attention. "Papa, what about *notre voiture?*"

"We sold our car, remember, buddy? It can't come to Vancouver." And good riddance to the old deathtrap that had already been on its last legs when I bought it used three years ago.

"*Ça me manque.*" Mo pouts. That facial expression is all me.

"I know you miss it, but we'll get a new one in Vancouver." If we can afford it. Maybe Errol has a car? Mo likes cars. When he was a baby, driving with him in his car seat was the only way I got any peace some nights.

"How far is Vancouver?"

"Far," I grit out.

"*Papa est grincheux,*" Monet grumbles, arms crossed over his narrow little chest, feet kicking the air as he slouches low in the seat beside me. I pat his hair. The French adjective stings, the way they always do since I moved here and had to get used to gendering myself that way. At least he used the masculine. Monet picks up on his mistake, he usually switches to English for words that don't have a neutral option. "*Désolé, Papa.* I meant grumpy."

"I know, and I'm sorry too, Momo. Lots on my mind." The rest of the shuttle ride passes in blessed silence. When we get to the terminal, I wrestle our bags and Mo's booster to the check in kiosk. I'm glad to check our suitcases through to Vancouver, even as the hefty extra baggage fees they charge make me wince. I make sure Mo has his tablet, headphones, charger and a couple snacks stashed in his little backpack.

We make it to the security check. They wave us through to a line with other parents and young kids. The security guy side-eyes my ID, then me, then my ID again. I hold my breath, ready to out myself, if he demands it. I got the marker changed when I started presenting masculine after retiring from hockey. Quebec made it easy enough. The hardest part was asking an old teammate to sign an affidavit about my identity. Still, the photo on my ID is several years old. Even after years on low dose testosterone and surgery to masculinize my chest, I don't always pass as a cis guy. The last hitch I need to deal with today is a scene at the airport over my gender presentation. Then the guy in his imposing uniform glances at Mo clinging to my hand, and lets it go with a, "have a pleasant flight, sir."

I cringe at the sir, though it stings less than when strangers defaulted to ma'am, and thank him. We make it to our gate and now we've got an hour to kill before our flight boards. I hand Monet his tablet to keep him occupied and buy us coffee and juice from the nearby kiosk. We sit with our drinks to wait.

"Papa?" Monet asks.

"Yeah?" I say.

"Will Daddy like me?" Monet shatters my heart again.

Fuck. "Errol is going to adore you, Monet. I promise. *Il t'aimera fort comme le ciel, mon chou.*"

"*Ouais?*"

"You can count on it."

"Papa?"

"Yeah?"

"Will he love you, *aussi?*"

I laugh at that. "I don't know. It's okay if he doesn't. I

hurt him pretty bad, Mo. Try not to borrow trouble, *mon petit chou*." Excellent advice, if only I could take it myself. Monet settles in to watch his show with his bright green headphones over his ears and his head leaned against my side. I let myself have a quiet freak out before texting Errol to be sure he's meeting us at the airport when we land.

I kick myself for sending the text. It's still before six here, making it not even three in the morning for him. I resist the urge to send followup texts apologizing for the first one. Then I put my phone in airplane mode to avoid temptation.

Monet and I watch a movie once we get in the air. They make us buy the airline earbuds because of some arcane regulations against over the ear headphones. The price makes me wince, but I pay it to have a peaceful flight. Mo grumbles that the buds hurt his ears, but the movie keeps him distracted. The touch screens embedded in the seat backs have games, and he cajoles me into playing a few rounds before zonking out for the last couple hours of the flight. I stare at the animated airplane making its way back toward the home I left behind when I was still half a kid myself. Mo was with me on that life altering flight, too. Barely showing under the baggy sweaters I wore, even through the heat of summer to hide the pregnancy.

God, this whole move is a walk down memory lane over shattered glass. This is why it's taken me seven years to come clean. It's going to be hard. So hard. Errol deserved better than I could give him back then. But I'm doing this because Mo deserves everything I can give him, including a relationship with his other dad. No matter how much facing my past is going to suck.

CHAPTER 3

Errol

They don't let you as far into the baggage claim area as I remember anymore, so I have to stand behind the barriers, scanning the crowd for Rene and Monet. Two faces so achingly familiar and utterly alien at the same time. Rene was eighteen when they left home. We were still teenagers. I know they've changed since I saw them last.

Every time I look at my single picture of Monet, I see more pieces of Rene, and then more of me. Mo looks so much like us. Ren's impish smile. My lanky build. Ren's mischief-filled eyes. My dark hair that won't take a curl no matter how hard I try or how much heat I apply. I'd kept it long enough at uni to play around with different styles for my drag persona, Shadow. That's in my past though, and my hair is shorter now. The kid in the picture could be my future.

I didn't think it was possible to love someone I've

never even met, but it seems I already do. I haven't told anyone about Monet, yet. There hasn't been time to process how I feel about the news, let alone share it.

I've only had a little over a day to prepare to boldly go into this parenting thing. I spent the morning preparing for Rene and Mo to move into my place. I turned my office into a bedroom for a little boy, jammed all my office things into my bedroom, and cobbled my dining nook into an enclosed room for my ex. They'll need their own space.

As I transformed my home to welcome Mo and Rene into it, I had so many questions and no one to ask. Did you need to childproof the electrical outlets for six-year-olds? I almost texted Emil to check, he's the kid expert in our group, but then I just googled it. If I told Emil, he'd want to tell Pia. Then Laura would get upset if I left her out of the loop, and Laura can't keep her mouth shut about good news.

This *is* good news. The fact I didn't know sooner is still devastating, but I can't change the past. All I can do is move forward with Monet in my life. And by extension, Rene.

The crowd of travelers from Rene's flight floods into the baggage claim. People around me are ignoring the signs to stay back and wait for your loved ones to leave the secure area. A loud alert announces that the conveyor of baggage is starting. It jerks into motion with a rattle as bags drop through a chute to make their way around.

People rush to grab their things and clear out of the area. The crowd thins. I still don't see Rene. And then I do. They're holding Mo on one hip, whispering into his ear. They point toward me, say something to the kid, and set him down. He squints at me. I wave, heart in my throat.

Mo glances back at Rene, who shoos him toward me. Monet jogs across the distance separating us.

I crouch down to greet him, wondering if I should open my arms to hug him or if that's too much. I want to hug my kid. But he seems unsure, so I keep my arms to myself. Monet pauses just out of arm's reach and gives me a shy smile and a wave.

"*Salut, Papa dit que...* pardon, Papa says you're my daddy and you don't speak French."

"*Seulement un peu d'école, mon chou*. You're Monet, right?" I ask.

Monet wrinkles his little button nose, but he nods. "You can call me Mo. Only my teachers call me Monet. Can I hug you?"

"Of course," I open my arms and almost get bowled over when the kid flings his entire body into the hug. I hold him and he wraps his arms around my neck so tight I think he could hang off me if I stood. I wrap my arms around him and fight back tears. He's real. This is all real. I have a bilingual six-year-old son who gives the world's most incredible hugs. I crouch there, holding him and breathing in his presence. Monet seems content to hug me for now, so I hold on tight.

It seems like no time at all has passed when his papa joins us, pushing a cart piled high with bags. "I need to get his booster seat from the bulky item area, you okay with him for a minute longer?" Rene asks, as though this isn't our first conversation as co-parents. Our reunion after seven years and the harsh words that ended our friendship. The possibilities in that simple exchange dampen my roiling anger at everything they took with them when they left without giving me the chance to know everything I was losing. I focus on the kid clinging to me.

It's not like I can vent my anger at Mo's papa in front of our son. It's between us and it should stay that way.

I take in Rene, standing in front of me. They seem nervous. Or is it he now? I'll have to ask when we get a minute to chat. They used to dress more androgenous when we were young. They still have shoulder length hair, wavy locks I still want to run my hands through. Hockey flow, they called it before. There's stubble on their cheeks now. No evidence of the curves they hated under the Habs jersey they're wearing.

"Of course," I say. Rene flashes me a tight smile and a nod, then strides off to get Mo's car seat.

Mo releases my neck and takes a step back. He regards me with a serious expression. "Do you have a car?"

"I do, it's parked outside. You can see it when your papa has all your things. Do you like cars?"

"Yeah. I like fast ones. Papa calls our car a lemon, even though it's brown, not yellow. My friend Laurent's dad drives a fancy convertible. When I'm big, I'm going to fix cars," Mo says, then his face falls and his eyes get all teary. "Our old car, I guess. It's not ours anymore. Papa said we can't bring everything here. We shipped my toys and stuff, though."

"Moving is hard, huh, kiddo? Tell me some other things you like?" I ask, hoping to distract him. The tactic works. He perks up as he lists off his favorite things.

"Dinosaurs. And sparkles. Papa said if I behaved during the move we could get a Switch. Do you have a Switch? I want to get *Battle Fox*. Laurent has it and we can play online if I get a copy, too."

"I do. Did your papa tell you what I do for a living?" I ask. Is it normal to be proud and terrified that my kid already knows how to connect with people online?

Proud that he's tech savvy, and he wants to play the game I helped make to stay in touch with his friend. And terrified about all the potential dangers he's nowhere near ready for online. Does Rene let him go online unsupervised? Do I get a say in whether that behavior continues?

"Papa said you make art," Mo says.

"Yeah. I make art for fun, but my job is making video games," I tell him. Mo's eyes widen, round as saucers.

"What games?" he demands.

"The studio I work for makes *Day Dreamer* and *Battle Fox*."

"You made *Battle Fox*? That's so cool! Laurent is going to love that when I tell him. Papa said we can call him later. What's it like? Do you draw the characters? Can I come see your work?"

I chuckle at Mo's enthusiasm. Glad he doesn't seem intimidated by me or too standoffish.

"Slow down with the questions, *mon petit monstre*, let Daddy get a word in," Rene admonishes Mo, ruffling the kid's hair as they return with a booster seat. They add it to the stacked luggage cart.

"Sorry," Mo apologizes with a glance toward Rene.

"No worries, kiddo. I work in production. Meaning I tell the artists and programmers who make the game what to do and keep everything running smooth. I can take you in to visit the studio sometime. Probably on a weekend, so we aren't disruptive. I can draw you a *Battle Fox* picture, but I can also get my friend Pia to paint some characters on your wall. They came up with the concept art for the game."

"Wow! Really? That's so cool! My favorite character is Ollie Owl, can your friend draw me an Ollie?"

I laugh, Laura is going to shit a brick when she sees that

damn owl on my walls. "Absolutely, Mo, whatever you want." I agree. He beams his gap-toothed grin at me and I'm already wrapped around his little finger. I could get used to this parenting gig.

CHAPTER 4

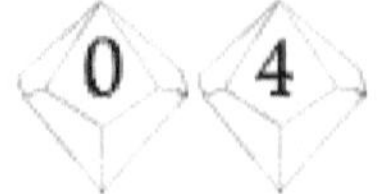

Rene

I watch Errol surreptitiously as he ruffles Mo's hair, then straightens to his full height and grabs the baggage cart. God, if that isn't an apt visual metaphor for our entire relationship, such as it is, I don't know what is. Me crashing into his life with a towering mound of baggage, and Errol shouldering it all like it's nothing. I swallow the lump that thought brings to my throat. I can handle this, for Mo's sake.

"Hold your papa's hand when we go outside, there's lots of cars," Errol instructs, like he's always been there at my side doing this with Mo. Errol pushes the cart toward the exit and I trail after him with Mo holding my hand.

"Do you have to pee before we leave?" I ask.

"No," Mo says. "I'm hungry."

"We can stop for food," Errol offers. "What do you like to eat?"

"Soup."

"Mo," I chastise him, but Errol smiles.

"I know just the place. Do you like pork?" Errol asks.

Mo wrinkles his nose. "Chicken."

"Okay, they have chicken too. And noodles. Big long tasty ones you can slurp, what do you say?"

"Sounds tasty," Mo says.

"Good. Let's get everything in the car and we'll go eat. Then we can go home and you can get settled." Errol maneuvers the cart off the curb and across the pick up lanes to the short-term parking.

"We're living with you now?" Mo asks. I stifle the impulse to assure them both it's a temporary arrangement. I can't impose on Errol forever.

"That's right," Errol agrees.

"Papa, are you and Daddy going to share a room? Marie-Claire's dads share."

"That's something your daddy and I need to discuss, Momo," I hedge, then I mouth an apology at Errol over our kid's head. Errol gives me a rueful look.

"Out of the mouths of babes, huh? Come on, my car's over here," Errol leads us to a newer model sedan. I help Mo into the backseat to wait. Errol loads our stuff into the trunk and I get Mo's booster installed, then strap the kid into it. By the time Mo is ready, Errol is shutting the trunk.

"I'll return the cart," I say, nervous now that it's sort of just Errol and me. Mo is watching us through his window.

"Wait, Rene," Errol grabs my wrist. He's not forceful about it, just a light touch to make me pause. I still cringe, old reflexes telling me a guy grabbing for me means danger. There's pity in his eyes now. "We should talk," he says.

"Yeah." I swallow hard, rubbing at the spot on my

wrist he touched. "I know. We will. But not in front of Mo, please? After he goes to bed tonight? He's exhausted from being up at the crack of dawn, so I'm sure he'll zonk out early and we can talk then. You can yell at me, clear the air, whatever you need to say. And uh, thanks for being so helpful with him."

"He's my kid," Errol says, almost affronted at my thanks. Like that's any guarantee he'd treat Mo well. In Errol's world, I suppose it is. Just when I thought I couldn't regret my stupid hormone driven teenaged poor choices any more, Errol proves me wrong.

"I'm sorry," is all I can say, and it's woefully inadequate. Errol gets in the car. I return the luggage cart. When I slide into the passenger seat, Mo is telling Errol all about his favorite cartoons. The kid slips into French when he gets excited. That will be a change for him. I have to meet with the local school to see about getting him a spot in their early French immersion program. They couldn't guarantee they had room for him when I reached out before the move. He's been in French daycare and preschool since he was an infant. I'm throwing so many changes at him with this move. I want to at least give him the familiarity of his language here. Classes with kids who won't make fun of him for slipping between French and English.

Errol drives us to a ramen place near his work. Mo slurps his soup enthusiastically and talks about his shows and games, and what he wants in his room. He tells Errol his favorite color is green, and he wants to be Ollie Owl for Halloween this year. He asks if Errol has green controllers for his Switch, and if not, can we get some, just for him to use. And Errol listens and asks Mo questions and looks at him like my kid is the most amazing little person he's ever met. And he is. Monet is my finest accomplishment. Some days I feel like he's the only right decision I've made in my adult life.

Errol used to watch me like that; like I was precious. I have no right to crave Errol's desire. I burned that bridge. Heck, I dynamited the bridge then set fire to the river it was crossing. It would be amazing, though, if the three of us could form an actual family.

After food, Errol takes us to his place. It's a cute little townhouse in Burnaby that his folks bought as an investment property when Errol moved to Vancouver for university. On the drive over he mentioned they gifted him ownership when he graduated from university. Considering the cost of real estate in the city, that was some gift. The place is the same as I remember from visiting him when he was still in school, the decor is more grown up now, though.

Errol and I bring in the suitcases, Mo carrying his backpack as he walks between us up the pavers to the door. Errol points to the tenant's entrance off to the side, and explains that the top floor is an apartment he rents out to students. Mo and I will live with him on the bottom floor which has two bedrooms and a den.

Errol lets us inside and gestures to the open living area. "Here's the living room, there's the Switch and the TV. Kitchen is in the back, laundry is in the washroom," he points to the room in question. Then he leads us past his bedroom. It looks disarrayed with the bed shoved into a corner to make room for a desk with a box full of computer parts and office supplies sitting on top.

The desk blocks access to the closet and more boxes of art stuff are shoved in the corner near a door that must lead to a master bathroom. I'm not sure how to feel about the obvious evidence he moved his office into his bedroom to make space for Mo and me.

"This is Mo's room," Errol gestures to the second bedroom. It's a good size, like the first, but without an en suite. "I wasn't sure what you liked, so it's basic for now. We can paint it green and get you some dinosaur stuff, maybe cool bedding? Whatever you want, Mo."

There's a twin bed with a matching dresser and bookshelves with nothing on them inside. Errol went out and got furniture for my kid. Our kid. Mo grins.

"Dinosaurs sound good. And Ollie Owl. Don't forget you promised Ollie Owl," Mo says, bouncing on his toes as he examines the space.

"Yeah, I'll call my friend about it tonight, alright?" Errol says.

"Alright. Where's Papa sleeping?" Mo asks as he notices there's only the one narrow bed.

"That's something your papa and I need to discuss, will you be alright unpacking your things for a bit?" Errol asks.

"Yeah. I want to find my toys," Monet upends his backpack onto the bed. For once, I don't nag him not to make a mess. Whatever lets him feel comfortable here is fine for now. I leave his suitcases by the dresser for him.

"We'll be here, call for us if you need anything," I kiss his temple. Mo tolerates the affection, but he's already absorbed in organizing his stuff. Errol and I leave Monet to explore his new room.

Errol leads me around the corner. There's an alcove that opens off the kitchen with a makeshift wall separating it from the rest of the house.

"The realtors called it a den. It's more of a dining nook, but I partitioned it off with bookshelves and a pressure rod for the curtain. So you'll have a modicum of privacy and storage space." Errol gestures to the flimsy partial wall blocking the room off from the rest of the home. "We can install something more permanent long term. There's a futon and a dresser. If you need anything else, we can—"

"You didn't have to do all this for us," I cut him off.

"I want to know my son, Rene. So, yeah, I did. I don't want you to live somewhere else with him, I don't want to miss any more of his life. I can take this room, if you require more privacy."

"Why are you being so fucking nice, Errol? You're always so fucking composed and perfect and I... I fucked up."

"You did," he agrees with a measured nod, arms crossed over his chest. "And you obviously didn't do it to hurt me. Hurting you won't make anything better."

"Why aren't you mad?" I ask, not daring to hope I can repair what I broke.

"I'm livid." Errol says. He still doesn't look mad, even with his arms crossed and his posture rigid.

"Then, why?"

"Because, that little boy loves you." Errol tips his head toward Mo's room. "You've been his entire world, and I want to be a part of his life, so that means being part of your life, too."

"Okay."

"You still go by Rene?" he asks abruptly.

"Yeah." I rub at my arms, self-conscious of his attention.

"Still they/them?"

"Yeah."

"But you're his papa?" he asks with genuine curiosity,

not like he wants to trap me.

"Yeah. Still non-binary. Still prefer to present more masc. I'd rather get misgendered as him than her. And Papa or other variants of being called Mo's dad are about the only gendered terms that don't make my skin crawl."

"Okay," he says, nodding to himself with a finality that makes me want to reach for him. I long to draw this conversation out longer.

"Errol?" I ask, keeping my hands at my sides with an effort, nails dug into my palms to keep them away from my teeth.

"Yeah?"

"If I could go back—"

Errol shakes his head sharply. "Don't. We'll destroy ourselves with that game. We can talk more after he's asleep, like you said. You have unpacking, I need to tell some people I've got a kid now. I just wanted to be sure I'm not misgendering you when I tell them who you are to me."

"And who am I to you?" I ask, unsure what I want to hear.

"My kid's papa," Errol says simply. Then he turns and walks away.

I deserve for that to hurt. I can't imagine how I'd feel if he'd kept Mo a secret from me for years. But he wasn't the one who had to carry Monet. Face a medical system that defaulted to misgendering me and speaking to me in a language I had only the most tenuous grasp over. I was a silly kid to think I could handle everything on my own, but in my mind, it had been the only viable option.

My folks wouldn't have supported me through school if they knew about Monet. I needed their help to pay for what my scholarships didn't cover. Especially since

I didn't get a dime of the hockey money during my first year riding the bench while I carried Monet and recovered from delivering him. Tuition, rent and food weren't cheap. I couldn't work enough hours to make ends meet, play hockey at a collegiate level, and stay on top of my studies, let alone do all that with a colicky newborn. So I needed my parents' financial help to complete my degree.

It was a minor miracle the school let me stay on the team for my first season when I showed up pregnant. I couldn't play that year, but the athletic department worked with me to pay out of pocket. Deferred the scholarship until my second year without telling my folks details beyond a medical deferment. I got Mo into a subsidized daycare and I got connected with other student parents to work out childcare for the hours the CPE didn't cover and we made do.

Those first few years had been hell. I'd dialed Errol's number multiple times daily, only to delete it before calling him. By the time I didn't feel like I was drowning, Monet was a year old and it seemed too late to come clean about what I'd done.

I want to tell Errol all that. But he doesn't want to hear it. If I expect him to respect my choices, I owe him similar respect, so I don't argue or try to call him back. If he wants to hear more about why I made my choices, Errol will ask.

The tiny makeshift room Errol put together for me isn't much, but it's the most personal space I've had in years. Mo and I shared a tiny one bedroom unit with a trundle bed. Errol gave me this, even after everything I put him through. I unpack my bags. I can do this. Live in Errol's house and learn to co-parent with him without expecting anything more.

CHAPTER 5

05

Errol

Rene and Monet are both putting away their stuff. I have a slew of messages on my group chat from the gang. Mostly, they're dragging me for canceling on them. There's a con in town, and I was planning to go with the group, then join everyone for a video game day at Gui's place. Our first gathering since Theo got back from staying with his folks near Whistler post-surgery. It's out of character for me to cancel plans at the last minute, but Rene always was a seat-of-their-pants planner. Guess some things never change.

I hate to cancel with the gang, but Mo comes first now. He needed me to pick him and Rene up from the airport. Give them a stable place to live after the cross-country move upended his life and saddled him with a parent he's never known.

I haven't found the words to tell my friends about Mo yet, but now that he's here, they ought to know about him. I skim the new messages as I figure out how to have this conversation with my closest friends. There's some older messages from Max asking where everyone is while they were at the convention.

Gui made a comment about his red shirt cosplay being more fun if I'd been there with my Spock getup. That's been my go-to cosplay choice for when I don't have time or energy for anything more complex for a while now. I could mix things up, like Theo who refuses to do a repeat ever, but I'm not as into it as him. The latest message implies that they're back at Gui's and breaking out the games.

Theo: Errol, why don't you like fun anymore? Laura's missing her Spectral partner, we are kicking her ass without your attrition deck here to prop her up.

Laura: Screw off, Theo. I have perfectly good decks of my own. Next time we'll make Jude use his own deck and see how well you do.

Jude: But I enjoy using Theo's dick... I mean deck ;P

Max: Keep the flirting/foreplay out of the group chat. Some of us aren't disgustingly loved up :P

Gui: Yeah, bro, TMI. Theo is infecting your brain with his inappropriate jokes.

Theo: LOL, no. I swear he was already like that when I got him; I didn't break him.

Jude: Sorry.

Pia: Enough chatter, geez, we're all in the same room and we're texting instead of playing? What gives?

Theo: Well, all of us except Errol, the losing loser who is losing by missing out on being here with all us cool people ;p

Laura: Yeah, Errol, I've got some major side-eye for you. Where are you today?

Errol: You will not believe me.

I send a selfie to the chat. It's one I snapped of Mo and me at the ramen place earlier. My phone rings.

"Explain yourself!" Laura demands. I can hear the others in the background.

"Am I on speaker?" I check.

"Yes. Stop stalling, and explain the picture Errol Control Freak Dawes," Laura demands.

"That isn't my middle name. Can't a guy enjoy a nice bowl of ramen without getting the third degree, Laura?" I can't resist teasing her a little.

Laura makes a growling sound of frustration and then demands, "Explain the mini-Errol in the picture with you. Did you discover a long-lost sibling and now you have a nibling?"

"It's a long story," I delay the inevitable.

"Summarize," Laura insists.

"Rene, my ex, hasn't explained all the details, but Monet is my kid," I announce to the group.

They all talk at once, Pia's voice carries over the others. "How the hell have we been friends for seven years and you never mentioned having a kid?"

"I only found out a couple days ago," I say.

They greet that news with silence.

"That sucks, Errol," Gui says when it starts to get uncomfortable. "If you need anything, we're here for you."

"Thanks, I appreciate that. I might need Emil on speed dial," I joke weakly. "I had to research how to childproof my place for a six-year-old. Turns out there isn't a rulebook for this whole kid thing."

Pia laughs and laughs. "Emil is about the closest you can get to having a manual to ask," she says. Then, sobering, they add, "I'll tell him about the kid, if you don't mind? He's kind of tetchy about children right now. He'll be happy for you; we're all happy for you, but the meds for kid number 2 make him into a monster. He's not as miserable as before having Rain, at least."

"How's that going?" I ask.

"It's going. You need to introduce us to Monet. Not going to lie, it will be nice to have another parent in the group to commiserate and split babysitting with," Pia says.

"Sounds good. On that note, I sort of promised him you would paint *Battle Fox* art on his bedroom wall. Maybe you all could come over next weekend to meet him and help us decorate?" I suggest. A week should give Mo time to settle in before I invite everyone to meet him. I hope. He seems to have accepted me well enough so far. He was so well behaved at the restaurant.

"Sure, I can do that for your little man, I owe you after all the babysitting you've done. Which characters does he like?" Pia asks.

"Laura, you can't judge my kid on his video game preferences," I hedge.

"Oh, my god, your kid is a monster who likes Ollie Owl? Seriously?" Laura teases. I'm pretty sure it's teasing, anyway. She despised modeling the owl last minute, but her work came out fantastic despite all her griping about it.

"Guess my kid just has good taste, you did such an amazing job that he couldn't resist even an evil owl's charms," I quip.

"It's a pretty cute owl," Jude agrees.

"Traitor," Laura growls. "Traitors, the lot of you. All kidding aside, though, we'll throw together a party for next weekend. Give the kid some time to adjust before we overwhelm him. Tell us what you all need so we can shower you and the kid with gifts to welcome you to being a dad."

"Bit late for a baby shower," I say dryly, but I'm touched by the gesture.

"Don't be a putz. Baby or not, the kid needs stuff, right?" Pia says.

"Pretty sure he already has stuff, it's not like he's appearing out of the ether," I say.

"What about your ex? If you're painting the walls, does that mean this Rene dumped the kid on you?" Max asks, his tone accusatory. It takes me a minute to realize he's upset because he's being protective of me.

"No." I push up my glasses. "It's, uh, complicated. Like VentureQuest, the second edition levels of complication."

"So complicated they are going to redact it and replace it less than a month after release?" Theo lets out a low, impressed whistle. "That *is* complicated."

"Can you give us the bare bones?" Laura asks.

"Rene and I dated through high school. We broke up after their graduation. They went to McGill for university, and we lost touch. Now, they're back in BC for a hockey coaching job. They needed a place to live, and I offered to let them move in with me so I can get to know my son," I summarize.

"Gotcha," Laura says. "You can give us the detailed version Monday at work over lunch."

"Sounds good. I'll let you all get back to game day. Laura, kick their asses at Spectral for me."

"Sure thing, they're going to experience the heart of my cards. Good luck with the kiddo," Laura says.

"Congrats on being a dad and all," Pia adds.

The others call out a jumble of congratulatory statements. Theo sings a couple lines from a song about being a dad, and Jude cracks a joke about calling him Daddy. Gui groans about that, Max jeers.

I roll my eyes at them. They can exasperate the heck out of me, but I love them like family. "Thanks, children. Obviously you've all been doing your best to prepare me for this day. I ought to thank you."

"Hey!" Theo complains.

"If the shoe fits," I shoot back.

"Oh, does the kid need shoes?" Theo purposely mishears me. "Get his sizes, if he needs stuff. My mom and sister are in town shopping for clothing for Sky this weekend. Guess there's a bunch of back to school type sales going on? Maybe we can pick up stuff for Mo, too?"

"Thanks, Theo. I'll text you about that when I have a better idea what he needs. Talk to you later."

I hang up before they can draw me into anymore banter. It's nice to know they all support me, though. I hum to myself as I get to work reassembling my office in the limited space within my bedroom. I shove the dresser inside the closet. Not ideal, but it fits and gives me a place for my desk near an outlet, so that will have to do.

Once the furniture is situated, I get the desk organized with my computer and art supplies set up on top of it for my drawing commissions. Rene knocks on my door as

I'm wrapping up the final little details.

"Hey, got a minute?" Rene asks, shifting from foot to foot.

"Yeah, I'm done in here. What's up?" I ask.

"Mo's napping. I figured we could have that chat?"

"Do six-year-olds still nap?" I ask, curious.

Emotions flash across Rene's face, central among them something suspiciously like regret. They give a weak chuckle. "Not usually. Not Mo, anyway. But it's been a long day. I'll wake him if he's out for more than an hour or he won't sleep at bedtime."

"Want coffee?" I offer, moving toward the door. Rene steps back to give me room.

"I, uh, don't do well with caffeine after noon."

"Wine, then? I could use a drink after the past few days," I say with a self-deprecating chuckle.

Rene hesitates, their eyes haunted. I could kick myself for suggesting booze as a coping mechanism, knowing their past. They nod. "Okay. One glass. Do you have any rosé?"

"You still like it sweet, huh? Laura has similar taste, she might have left a bottle in the fridge."

"Oh. Um. Is Laura...?" Rene trails off to let me fill in who Laura is to me.

"My friend. I'm not seeing anyone," I say. We walk to the kitchen. Rene leans against my counters and I get out the wine and two glasses.

"Good. Or, I mean, not good. It's just, that, uh, makes it easier. Not having to explain why your ex is moving in with you. Sorry. I should've asked if that would be an issue before barging back into your life." Rene runs their fingers through their hair in a nervous gesture.

"It's fine, Rene." I sigh. "There hasn't been anyone else

since you. Not anyone worth mentioning."

"I'm sorry."

"Stop apologizing. Tell me what you've been doing." I pour the wine and slide a glass to Rene.

"Thanks." They take a sip. "Not much. School, work, hockey, raising Mo. That about covers it."

"Do your parents know about him?" I press.

"No. We don't talk. They washed their hands of me when I went pro instead of getting a proper job that can pay the bills," they say with a bitter twist of their lips. Rene's family was never close, but it still can't have been easy to cut ties.

"Once my folks know, word might get back to them," I warn. Our parents were never friends, but we grew up in a small town and gossip travels. Even with Rene's folks having moved away.

Rene shrugs. "It's fine. I'm not hiding his existence. Not anymore. I never meant for it to go this far. I don't want them in his life, but if they find out he exists, it is what it is."

"Why *did* you hide him?" I ask.

"You want a play-by-play?" They swirl the wine in their glass, avoiding eye contact.

"Yes."

"At first? I figured I was just late. And then I realized we never got around to buying condoms when you were visiting for spring break," Rene takes a deep breath and shrugs. "The whole situation terrified me. I had no idea what to do. You were away at school. I wanted to tell you, but you were so happy at UBC. You were figuring out who you are, making art, and connecting with people. I couldn't take that away. I ran off to school early because I dreaded what would happen if my folks found out about

Mo. When I left, I thought if you never knew he existed then it wouldn't hurt. If I decided not to... then when I couldn't go through with losing my last connection to you, how could I tell you? After what I said?"

"So you hid him instead?" I try not to make it an accusation.

"Yeah, well, eighteen-year-old Rene made stupid choices," Rene says. They drop their face into their hands.

"And you spent the past seven years doubling down on that stupidity, Rene. That's what I'm mad about. That you never reached out. Never gave me the chance to be there to support you."

"You could have reached out to me, if you cared," Rene says, but it's more defeated resignation than a real argument.

"I cared. You told me I wasn't welcome in your life." I cross my arms, I don't want to be mad, but every time I think about it, I feel the sharp ache of loss more acutely.

"You're right. I can't ask you to forgive me, but can we try to get along as friends for Mo's sake?" Rene pleads.

"We can try." I swirl my wine and take a sip. Rene mirrors the gesture.

"So, what have you been up to?" Rene changes the subject when the silence feels like it's growing teeth.

"Like I told Mo, I make video games. I got into drag at UBC after my first year, performed a lot as a student, that's where I met my friends Pia, Emil, and Gregor. They have a kid now too, though I guess Mo is too old for playdates with infants, huh?"

"A little, yeah. Last time he was around babies he started asking for a brother," Rene says, nose wrinkling in distaste.

"Yeah, that's uh, not likely on my side," I say.

"Tell me about it. I love him to pieces, but pregnancy was hell." Rene barks out a harsh laugh after that pronouncement. There's a world of hurt in that laugh, and I want to comfort them. I put a hand on their elbow.

"I missed you," I say, because it's true. The past seven years have clearly been hard on them. I can be so mad I want to scream and still realize that Rene didn't do this to hurt me. That their decisions hurt them, too. Maybe even hurt them more than me, if in different ways.

"You have no idea how many times I was this close to calling you," Rene admits, holding up two fingers pinched together. They shove the barely touched wine glass away.

"I really wish you had. But that's in the past, now. We should put it behind us and focus on building a new partnership, for Mo. I'd like you both to live with me as long as you'd like. We can figure out something more permanent for your room. My upstairs tenants are students who graduated from UBC last spring. Their lease ends in a few weeks. Since they aren't renewing this year, I can hold off on finding new tenants, if you think you'd want to have more space."

"I don't mind living with you. Like a family." Rene shrugs.

"No 'like' about it. We might not be together, but we share a kid. That makes us family. We'll figure out the whole co-parenting thing. You'll have to help me out, since you've got a bit of a head start." I joke. Rene winces at the reminder, and I shake my head. "I didn't mean that as an accusation."

"Okay. So, we live together, raise our kid together. Do you date? Hook up?"

"Very rarely. You know me," I say. Rene *does* know me,

even if it's been years since we were close. That was why they'd been able to eviscerate me so succinctly when we broke up.

"I didn't mean what I said that day." Rene won't meet my eyes. "All of it was a lie."

They'd accused me of being frigid, among worse epithets, even though they knew I was insecure about being perceived that way. Worse, they'd done it in front of everyone. My folks knew I was panromantic, but our families and friends didn't need to hear details about our sex life dragged out and used to inflict maximal damage.

I sigh, shoving my glasses up my nose. "It wasn't okay. But I understand why you did it."

"Yeah. Sorry. God, Errol, you have no idea how sorry I am." Rene glances at me, anguish in their eyes.

"I'm getting the picture." I say dryly, hoping to soften the mood.

"Would you ever want—no, nevermind." They shake their head, like they want to dislodge whatever thought they left unsaid. "So, if I, uh, meet anyone, I'll find somewhere else to bring them, yeah?" they suggest.

"This is your home, too," I say. The idea of Rene with someone else makes my stomach twist, but I'm not dating them and they have a right to find happiness. Or just have sex, if they want.

"Our home that we share with our kid. I don't bring hookups home when Mo might be around," Rene says. I can't say I'm unhappy to hear it.

"What about boyfriends or joyfriends?" I pry.

"I don't date." Rene shakes their head.

"Not at all?" That surprises me.

"You're my only ex, too, Errol."

"Well. That's... huh." I rub at my neck, uncomfortably aware that we're both hung up on that first love we shared. It can't be healthy. But there was a reason I'd called them my imzadi when we were together. And it was about more than using a cool word from my favorite show. Rene was my beloved, my first in every sense, my soulmate. I still want them in my life, now that they're back, but I'm not sure what I want that to look like.

Rene is watching me, looking at my lips with a rosy glow of attraction. I turn to the fridge before they can act on that longing glance. Putting the past behind us does not mean picking up where we left off years ago, even if a part of me still loves them and remembers what it felt like to want them in ways I've never wanted anyone else.

"What does Mo like for dinner?" I ask, head buried in the fridge. It's not too early for supper, and the meal I have planned to welcome them home takes a while to prep.

"He's not too picky, for a kid. I never have time to cook much fancy, though," Rene says, sounding sheepish.

"Well, I've got ingredients to do Mom's chicken parm with roast broccoli," I say, trying to sound casual. I glance over my shoulder at them.

"My favorite," Rene murmurs, flashing me a heart-breakingly sweet smile.

"I remember," I reply as I turn to pull the ingredients from the fridge. So much for trying to create distance and discourage any rekindling of old flames.

CHAPTER 6

0 6

Rene

It's weird being around Errol again. He acts normal, but he has always been good at wearing a mask to hide his genuine emotions. It stings that he doesn't take that mask off around me anymore. Still, putting the past behind us doesn't erase how badly I broke his trust. I'll have to earn it back, if that's even possible.

Mo adjusts to the move better than I expected. He enjoys having his own room here instead of the trundle bed in our old apartment. He loves playing with Errol's video games and the action figures arrayed on shelves in the living room.

I saw the way Errol bit his lip about letting the kid play with them at first. Mo saw it too. He's perceptive, our kid. He apologized for not asking permission first. Errol blew out a heavy breath, ruffled Mo's hair and got down the ones Mo couldn't reach to arrange them on the lower shelves for him.

Errol fits into place with Mo and I. Most nights since the move, he cooks and I clean the dishes and put away the leftovers. He rough houses with Mo and sits with us for whatever shows or movies Mo chooses without acting bored. When Mo chooses to stream Star Trek, the two of them nerd out over it, making my heart ache with memories of Errol as a teenager waxing eloquent about his favorite show.

Errol doesn't comment when Mo slips into French with me. He just grins and tries his best to answer if Mo forgets to switch back to talk to him. Mo's pretty good at code switching, unless he's too caught up to pay attention to what he's saying.

Errol plays games with the kid. He doesn't let Mo win, but he is careful not to beat him by a wide margin or too often, staving off frustration-fueled tantrums at not winning. Errol acts sweet with Mo in a way I've never seen him with anyone else. It makes me feel all mushy inside to watch Errol read our son his bedtime stories. Errol kisses Mo's forehead and answers his endless questions about why he has to put on pajamas, brush his teeth and sleep.

One week into living with Errol, and this new life already surpasses everything I dared to hope for when I got the wild idea to apply for work in BC.

Now, it's Friday night and I'm sitting at Errol's kitchen counter with my ancient laptop after putting Mo to bed. I've got a serious problem. I didn't consider how much more expensive childcare is here when I planned this move. My new job starts in another week, and I have no one to watch Mo. No friends, or former teammates, or school friends. No family I can trust. Errol's folks might babysit. I would trust them, but they still live in the tiny mountain town nearer to Kelowna than Vancouver, where Errol and I grew up. Worst case, I can get permission to bring Mo to sit in the team office for a few days, but that will get old fast.

As worry creeps up on me, it's the strangest thing to realize that this isn't all on me. I have another adult to turn to for help. An adult who still isn't home.

I chew my nails and glance at the clock. Past ten. Errol said not to wait up, that his gaming group goes late when they meet. He also said he planned to go out for drinks with them after their game. I can talk to him about it when he gets home. If he's not too drunk.

I sigh. The place seems too quiet with Mo asleep and Errol out with his friends. Even when Errol retreats to his room in the evening to work on art commissions, there's a quality to his presence in the space. The warm glow of light from his room and the soft beat of quiet instrumental music that he listens to when he draws. How am I already so used to Errol being around? Doesn't matter. This can't be whatever it is my foolish heart is set on seeking here with Errol.

Mo won't need me again until morning, and I don't have any plans for tonight beyond figuring out childcare, which isn't going to happen at this hour. Restless, I dig in the freezer for Errol's ice cream. I top it with the syrup and whipped cream he brought home for Mo. I assuage my guilt over helping myself to Errol's fancy name brand groceries with the mental promise that I'll buy him more when I get paid. I return to the computer and minimize the tab with all the daycare listings. Any of them would cost me a modest mortgage payment every month to take care of Mo while I work. Instead, I open a new window to stream a cooking show where the biggest controversy is whether you can trust a person who doesn't like cheese. Answer: you can't.

If I'm trying to stay awake until Errol gets home, just to see him, and hear him say goodnight, and allow myself the fantasy that this can become something more, well, no one has to know that but me and my ice cream.

CHAPTER 7

0 7

Errol

Tonight is our first game session since Theo returned from his surgery. His recovery process was rough for a while, but he seems to be back to his usual chipper self. We're all just arriving at our usual conference room, and he's taking part in Eye-On's dollar donation Friday. The studio lets employees wear PJs to work on the first Friday of every month if they chip in toward the cause of the month. Theo almost always takes advantage of the opportunity, and this time he's got on a dinosaur pajama. Complete with a ridiculous stuffed tail that thwacks me in the thigh when he turns excitedly to share another off the wall wedding idea with Jude. His new fiancé, as of a few hours ago. As if the massive grins on their faces, and Jude's shiny new ring, weren't enough of a hint, they blasted the group chat with inane marriage GIFs all afternoon. Theo has already demanded we all prepare to be a part of their big day.

Now Theo is babbling about renting a castle and playing VentureQuest with all our friends after the ceremony. Or better yet, having the actual vow exchange in-game. With one of us getting ordained to act as the cleric if this rented castle is some place that allows that. An in-game wedding sounds a tad over the top, even for Theo. The rest of the idea might be fun, though travel costs can get prohibitive. I stop myself from getting too deep into figuring out logistics; it's doubtful they'll have their wedding out of the province. Unless it's in LA, where Jude's family lives. Either way, planning their wedding can wait until after tonight's game.

"Watch where you stick your appendage," I complain, knowing it will make Theo cackle like a 12-year-old. That ought to distract him from off the wall wedding ideas. Sure enough, he laughs and turns to smack the tail into Jude.

"Hey, Jude, want to check out my turgid appendage?" Theo waggles his eyebrows comically. He smacks the tail against Jude again.

"Not at work, Thee, your appendage is all mine," Jude shoves the tail away. Then leans in to kiss Theo.

"Get a room," Max jeers, rolling his eyes at the pair.

We get to the gameplay shortly thereafter. It ends up being a quick session. Theo flags after a few hours, still rebuilding his stamina while healing from his surgery. We call it an early night, and that's fine with me. Pia insists we all have to go out for a beer after the game, to celebrate Jude and Theo's big news. We toast them and cover their drinks for the night, and it's nice. It's even nicer to have people to come home to after I drop off Max and Laura at their respective homes. Even if Mo and Rene are both asleep when I let myself inside the house, I like knowing I'm not here alone.

I wake up to the sound of Mo and Rene laughing and talking in the kitchen. Mo's giggles fill me with warmth. I stretch under the blankets, making no move to rise. I only had one beer last night with my buddies, so I'm not hung over, but I am groggy after only a few hours of sleep.

When I got home last night, Rene was dozing on the couch. Their ancient brick of a laptop had displayed a Netflix screen asking if they were still watching. I'd covered them with a blanket and set the laptop on the table so it wouldn't fall and break. Then I stared at Rene's face, relaxed in sleep, for way too long. It took an effort of will to tear myself away from cataloging all the ways, large and small, they'd changed since I'd last kissed their lips.

The familiarity of studying their face while they slept hurt. They still have the little scar bisecting their eyebrow from falling off our bikes when we were fourteen. The freckles the summer sun always brought out remain sprinkled across their nose. The faded mark where they'd gotten an eyebrow piercing at sixteen, only to let it close up after their folks threw a shit fit about it. And there are new marks. The familiar line of their nose appears crooked now, from a break during their season of playing with the Canadiennes.

The stubble along their jawline is new, too. My facial hair had always fascinated them, back when we were dating. I have fond memories of them laying on top of me. Rene gazing into my eyes, and just stroking my cheeks. The bristle of my patchy hair making little rasping noises against their fingers as they asked what it felt like.

Here I am, doing it again. Reminiscing about Rene isn't good for anyone. I can't return to being the naïve boy who never experienced heartache. No more than Rene can undo the years of being a young single parent struggling to survive.

Still, as I lay in bed listening to Rene make silly animal sounds while Mo laughs at them, I can imagine a future with more intimate moments like that. Moments I can share with the love of my life.

Sometimes I wonder if Rene is the only person in the world I'll ever love like this. It's silly. I fell for Rene over the course of our friendship. As natural as breathing, so that by the time I realized I was in love, it felt like I'd always loved Rene. It was only then that I'd started to notice them in a sexual way. The smile I loved was no longer just a sign my best friend was happy, it had become a smile I wanted to kiss.

If it happened with Rene, then it could happen again. If I ever let myself get that close to someone. Someone else. Thinking that shouldn't wrench my heart out like it does.

I reach for my glasses, settling them on my face before getting out of bed. I join my family for breakfast. We've got a busy day ahead and I want to make sure we're ready for the influx of guests when all my friends arrive.

As I enter the kitchen, I'm struck by the scene before me. Rene is at the stove pouring pancake batter into animal shapes, and Mo is watching while he bites the head off a vaguely dinosaur shaped pancake blob.

If this was one of Jude's sappy movies, I'd walk up behind Rene. Wrap my arms around them and kiss their cheek. Make them giggle and turn in my arms for a proper kiss. Mo would make the requisite grossed out noises of a kid embarrassed by his parents displaying affection. In some alternate reality, that family could be us.

Instead, I mumble a sleepy, "Good morning." Then I shuffle to the coffee pot and pour myself a mug. I sit beside Mo at the counter to watch Rene work.

"I'll take a chicken, if you're doing requests," I say.

Rene shoots me an evil eye, but says sweetly, "Whatever you want, stud."

The 'chicken' looks more like an egg. I snort in amusement. "Which came first?" The old inside joke between us slips out before I can catch myself.

Rene chokes on a suppressed laugh and gives me a broad wink as they deliver the punchline that always made us giggle as teenagers. "The rooster, obviously."

I laugh, and Rene joins me. Mo narrows his eyes at us. "That's not a very good joke. It doesn't make sense."

"Well, to be fair, I'm an artist, not a comedian," I joke. Rene snorts and rolls their eyes at the modified Star Trek line.

"Sorry, Momo. Do you have a better chicken joke for us?" Rene asks.

"Sure," he says with an eager nod. He swivels in his seat to face me. "Why did the chicken cross the road twice?"

"Why?"

"Because, he was a double-crosser!" Mo declares with a delighted giggle. I laugh with him and then he says, "Wait, I've got another one: why does a chicken coop have two doors?"

"One for in and one for out?" I suggest.

Mo shakes his head. "Nope, because if they had four doors, they'd be chicken sedans," he delivers the punchline through raucous laughter. And I chuckle again, half at the joke and half at how amused it makes him. Rene laughs along too, plating up the last batch of pancakes and then joining us at the breakfast bar to eat our meal.

Mo comments that the last few pancakes aren't animals. Rene says that they made theirs into hockey pucks, and Mo shakes his head at the answer.

"Daddy, tell Papa that hockey isn't an animal."

"It could be," Rene teases.

"You could at least use hockey mascots," I point out, which earns me a death glare from Rene.

"Oh, good idea! Next time can we do mascots, Papa?" Mo wriggles in his seat, excited at the suggestion.

"*Bien sûr, mon chou.*" Rene flashes me a wicked grin. "Daddy is a great artist, I bet he'd love to make you hockey logo pancakes."

"And for you, too?" Mo asks. Rene's face falls. They swallow hard and stuff their mouth full of pancakes to avoid answering.

"I'll make them for Papa, too," I agree, knocking my knee against Rene's under the table. We don't have to be involved romantically to treat each other with kindness. I might need to invest in kitchen gear if fatherhood involves being asked for custom pancake commissions, though. Rene did a darn good job for using a spoon and a measuring cup to draw shapes with the batter.

"Are you excited to play *Battle Fox* with Daddy's friends today?" Rene asks. I hope the gang doesn't overwhelm Mo. They're all so eager to meet my son, I'm sure he'll end up with a heap of gifts, but they can be a lot.

Mo wrinkles his nose and gives a careful nod as he licks syrup off his fork. He says, "I guess." Then takes another bite of his dinosaur.

"Most of them worked on *Battle Fox*," Rene reminds him, and he perks up.

"Oh, you mean Pia's going to draw my Ollie Owl today? I'm excited about that. I want to send pictures to Laurent. Can we video chat after breakfast?"

Rene bites their lip and glances at the clock. "How about we wait until later tonight? After Pia paints your mural, so you can show him."

"Okay," Mo pouts. He finishes his pancake and shoves his plate away. "Can I play Switch now?"

"One hour," I say, Rene and I had that discussion after the first time I gave the kid free rein for screen time. It only occurs to me belatedly that our video game day with the gang is going to go way over his screen time allotment. I guess today's party is an exception to the rule?

"You've got a special dispensation to play more during the party, but that's it, understood?" Rene says, confirming my thoughts. I'm glad we're on the same page.

Mo nods. "Yes, Papa."

"And wash your hands first," Rene adds, saving the matched pair of brand new green controllers I had to trawl every BestBuy in town to find from syrupy fingers. Mo runs off to wash up and I grin at Rene.

"We make a decent team, huh?" I nudge our elbows together.

"Yeah," Rene smiles at me, nudging back. We eat our pancakes to the sounds of Mo playing *Battle Fox* with his new green controllers. Then I make sure the house is in order for my friends when they arrive around noon. Mo pitches in to help me tidy his room for Pia to paint.

Pia arrives first with her men and their kid in tow. Emil has baby Rain strapped to his chest. Gregor is carrying a bag stuffed full of baby gear and Pia has their painting supplies.

"First things first, introduce us to the tiny Errol clone,"

Pia demands as they sweep past me into my house.

"Hi to you, too," I say, used to her abruptness.

"Hey, I'm here to do a free commission for the kid, so I should at least get to meet the client, right?" Pia declares, hands on their hips.

I sigh. "I'm happy to pay for your work, Pia."

Pia waves me away with a laugh. "Uh, no. You can pay me back for the cost of supplies, but I'm happy to give your kid a gift, Errol."

"Okay," I agree. I drop it for now, already planning out a charcoal portrait that I can do for Pia.

I have the perfect reference photo in mind. When Rain was a newborn, Pia had sent the group chat a snapshot of the baby sleeping between Gregor and Emil on their floor with their dog, Otis, in the background. I bet it would make a stunning black and white drawing. The texture of the charcoal will be ideal to capture the soft domesticity of the scene. And Pia can't say no once it's done. I've got enough photos of Pia to add her to the composition too, perhaps sitting with Otis. Make it a full family portrait.

"Hey, Errol," Emil says. He grabs Rain's little fist and moves it in a wave. "Raincloud says hi, too." The little munchkin has chubby cheeks and big bright eyes that gaze at me like I'm some alien creature. They make a burbling sound, then snuggle their face into Emil's chest.

"Good to see you. Is Rain being shy today?" I stroke a finger over their downy hair. Rain nuzzles against Emil, so I withdraw my hand.

"They're a grump, living up to the Raincloud moniker," Gregor supplies, clapping me heartily on the back. "Thanks for inviting us over."

"Anytime," I agree, then I lead my guests into the living room where Mo is playing with my action figures. Rene has disappeared. Hiding in their room from the strangers, or giving us space? I don't know, but I don't intend to pry.

"Hey, Mo, want to meet my friends?" I ask, going to crouch beside the kid.

Mo glances up and waves shyly at the new people. "Hi, I'm Mo. He/him."

That's something he must have gotten from Rene.

"Hiya, Mo. I'm Pia, she/they. And these two are my boyfriends. Emil and Gregor, both he/him. And our baby Rain, they/them until they tell us otherwise. I'm the person who offered to paint you an Ollie Owl. Your daddy says Ollie is your favorite *Battle Fox* character, is that right?"

"Yeah!" Mo nods. "I like when he wins, and he does this," Mo says, hopping to his feet to strike Ollie's victory pose from the game.

Pia grins at him. "Is that how you want him posed on the wall?"

Mo nods vigorously, "Yeah. I want him over my bed. Papa and I painted the walls green, so they'd be ready for you. Want to see?"

"Sure," Pia agrees. Mo takes their hand and tugs them to his room.

"Well, they hit it off," Emil observes as Mo chatters away with Pia about the art he wants.

"Seems that way. I'm going to put out snacks and we can order dinner when everyone is here. Can I grab you anything to drink?" I offer. Emil and Gregor follow me to the kitchen. I pull out the snack stuff I bought earlier in the week when I took Rene and Mo to get groceries. Chips, cookies, and a veggie platter, the latter because Jude has to be careful about eating the junk the rest of us take for granted. Won't hurt to model healthy snacks for Mo, either, come to that.

"Just water," Emil says, rocking Rain from side to side in the carrier.

"Water's fine for me, too," Gregor agrees.

"Want ice?" I ask as I grab them each a glass and fill it from the filtered water spigot on the fridge.

"Nah, that's fine," Emil says as I hand him his drink.

"No thanks," Gregor echoes him.

"Mind if I drink a beer?" I ask, grabbing one out of the rack I stuck in the fridge earlier.

"Nah, go for it." Emil waves off the question.

I crack open the beer and we migrate to the living room.

"How's the dad thing going?" Emil tips his head toward Mo's room to indicate the kid. He sits and removes Rain from the carrier. Gregor pulls a baby blanket and a couple of soft toys out of their diaper bag, arranging them on the floor. Emil lays Rain on their tummy and coos at the baby.

I sink down on the couch and grin at my friends doting over their kid. Do I look that goofy happy with Mo?

"It's amazing," I reply. "I'm still processing everything, but I love that little guy more than I'd have thought possible after a week.

"Glad to hear you are assimilating to the ways of parenthood," Gregor jokes.

"Resistance is futile, right?" I shoot back. Gregor chuckles.

"That's for sure," Emil agrees.

"In all seriousness, though, we've had a good week. Mo is well behaved and he's pretty good at *Battle Fox*, too. He's giving me a run for my money when we play."

"Theo and Gui are bringing their Switches so we can

have a big tournament," Gregor observes. He drags a stuffed fish across the blanket and Rain bats at it.

"Mo gets dibs on Ollie," I declare.

"From what I hear, that might make him Laura's primary target," Emil says.

"Laura will play nice with my kid if she wants to keep the taxi service going," I say wryly. I only half mean it. Giving Laura rides isn't a big deal. I enjoy the company at the end of our nights out. It makes the drive home less lonely. Although, with Rene and Mo waiting at home for me this past week, the familiar sense of oppressive emptiness that's always filled my home has vanished. Strange how fast everything can change.

Emil and Gregor chuckle. Gregor quips, "Does that mean Pia's got free rides lined up for a while after doing this painting?"

"Count on it," I agree, taking a swig of my beer. "So, how's life?"

"Not bad. I'm loving staying home with our little Raincloud. Just, uh, figuring out what we're doing once our parental leave runs out. I'm thinking I might not go back."

"Oh, were you thinking of staying home with Rain?" I ask.

"Sort of." Emil sighs. "I prefer working with younger kids. Like, preschool and early elementary age. Might apply at daycares again. It's just tough, not many masc daycare workers, you know?"

"That's too bad," I say.

"We're still figuring out the details of Emil staying home with Rain longer-term," Gregor adds.

"Yeah, we'll see how things develop. It'll be a few years before Rain can start school. Multiple daycare slots for two so close in age will just about cost more than I make. If this cycle goes well…" Emil trails off with a shrug. Huh. I hope he's exaggerating about the financial stuff, or else school teachers get paid less than I thought. Rene and I haven't talked about what to do with Mo when their job starts in a week. Surely, if it was that expensive to get daycare, they'd have mentioned the cost to me? I'll have to discuss that with Rene later.

"With the IVF?" I ask, not sure if I should, but Pia said the three of them were okay with us knowing they're trying for another kid.

Emil takes a deep breath and nods. "Yeah. I'm afraid to get my hopes up again. This is kind of my last ditch effort." He rubs a hand over his abdomen in the sort of unconscious gesture Pia used to do when they were carrying Rain. Gregor puts a comforting arm around Emil, giving him a quick squeeze. Emil forces a tight smile and teases Rain with one of their toys. The baby snatches the plush rabbit and stuffs it into their mouth with a pleased squawk.

"Sorry, I won't mention it again, if you'd rather not discuss it." I roll my beer bottle between my hands and pick at the label.

"No, it's fine. I just started taking the oral contraceptives. Seems ass-backwards, but they make you take them before the injections to stimulate follicle growth so they can harvest your genetic material. The hormones make me feel not great. Sorry," Emil says with a sheepish shrug. Gregor gives his back another comforting pat.

"Can confirm, you're an intolerable ball of feels on E," Pia calls from Mo's doorway, "but it's for a good cause and we love you anyway, sweetheart. Errol, can you come help us move some furniture, I want to be sure we're putting everything in the right spot."

"Gee, I can feel the love, Pea, thanks," Emil grouses, but he's smiling at them. Pia sticks out her tongue at Emil, then turns and flounces back into Mo's room, expecting me to follow.

I help Pia move Mo's bed so we can cover up the carpet around her work area with an old sheet. Mo wants to help move the furniture, so I let him stand in front of me and 'help'. His involvement makes me paranoid I'm going to drop the heavy bed frame on his little feet. He's so proud of himself for contributing that I can't begrudge the extra effort.

Pia smirks knowingly at me. "Look at you, moving furniture, like a boss," she teases, ruffling Mo's hair when we're done.

"I bet your baby will be a big helper too, when they're big like me," Mo says. "When my papa and daddy get me a brother or sister, they can be friends with Rain."

Pia stifles a laugh in their hand. Her eyes are dancing as she coughs and says, "I'm sure they would be. When Rain's a little bigger, you can teach them to play games, huh?"

"Yeah. I can teach them lots of stuff. Do you and your boyfriends speak French? Daddy doesn't so we gotta speak English for him," Mo chatters.

"Gregor speaks a little, I think his uncle was from Quebec," Pia replies as she contemplates the wall where the mural is going.

"Oh. Cool. Do you speak other languages?" Mo asks, mimicking the way Pia is regarding the wall.

"Just a little high school French. Emil's family spoke some Yiddish at home, I think," Pia says, glancing at Mo.

"What's that?" Mo asks, curiosity piqued.

"It's a language some Jewish people speak," Pia supplies.

"Is Emil Jewish?" Mo asks, all guileless innocence.

"Yeah. He's not observant, but he is." Pia nods.

"What's that mean?" Mo asks, looking confused.

"He doesn't follow the religious teachings, but being Jewish is still important to his identity," Pia says.

"Oh. Okay." Mo nods. "Papa says we got to respect people's religion, even if we don't agree with it."

"That's right," I agree. I'm not surprised to hear that's Rene's take on religious education. Knowing Rene, that was all they'd said on the matter. Not that I have much to add, neither of us grew up in a religious household.

"Daddy, can I go ask Emil about being Jewish?" Mo asks.

"Why don't you ask Emil permission before you start with the questions, hm?" Pia suggests brightly. If it was a sore spot, she wouldn't send the kid to ambush Emil. So, when Mo glances at me for permission, I nod and tell him it's fine. He scampers off to ask his questions.

"That won't upset Emil?" I double-check.

"Anything that gets his mind off the egg retrieval is a good thing," Pia says, digging through their supplies for something. "Besides, he's still not super observant, but he's been taking Rain to a reform temple the past few months. Reconnecting with that part of himself. He'll be happy to answer Mo's questions. And if I'm wrong, he'll redirect; you know how he is with kids."

Pia's right, Emil is a total softie with children. Mo will be fine.

"So, is there any chance you and his papa are going to give Rain a little playmate?" Pia jabs me in the ribs when I stand there staring at the wall.

"What? No!" I squawk, more flustered than the question merits. "We aren't getting back together. Mo knows that."

"Do you want to?" Pia asks as they sketch the design onto the wall using light pencil strokes.

I shrug. "Did I ever tell you why we broke up?"

"Just that you had an ugly breakup with your high school ex," Pia says.

"This stays between us?" I ask.

"Sure thing." Pia glances away from their work to flash me a sympathetic smile. "What happened?"

"I graduated high school the year before them. We made the distance work for my first year at UBC. We talked about them playing hockey here, but at the last minute they accepted an offer from McGill instead. I didn't know until they dumped me at their graduation party in front of half the town. They said... well, what they knew would hurt me most. Jabs at my being pan and demi, stuff that came as a total shock because I knew Rene didn't believe that shit."

"That's awful," Pia commiserates. Then she glances at me and I can see the 'but' coming a mile away.

"There isn't a but," I protest. "How can I trust someone who doesn't think I'm enough?"

"I'm not telling you to give Rene a second chance, Errol. But don't you think you deserve a chance to find love with *someone*?" Pia asks in a gentle tone.

I shrug. It's nothing I haven't heard before. It still stings coming from Pia. They're one of my closest friends. "You know I don't need sex to be happy, right?"

"I never mentioned sex." Pia points out, jabbing her pencil toward me. "Companionship is a valid reason to be in a relationship."

"That's what I've got all of you for," I joke.

Pia shrugs. "Sure, and you always will. But, with us all settling into romantic relationships, it changes things. Laura's been flirting with Alice, and Max is new to the group, but the rest of us are settling down. I don't want to push you toward anything you don't want, man. Just saying, don't let an unpleasant experience from when you were a teenager color what you let yourself experience now that you're an adult. Sounds like Rene was in a hell of a hard spot. It doesn't excuse what they said, but if they're anything like me, pregnancy is wild for dysphoria, yeah?"

"Yeah. We haven't discussed what it was like in detail, but they're more like Emil than you, dysphoria-wise," I say.

Pia nods. "Then I'm sure it sucked. So, cut them some slack for being young and scared. If you're thoroughly Rene-sexual or Rene-mantic, maybe that alone tells you whether you're ready to write off exploring more than co-parenting with them?"

I blow out a heavy breath and run my fingers through my hair as Pia continues to outline Ollie onto Mo's wall. "Yeah. It's not the breakup, or the running away. I get why they did those things. It's the fact I'll never get the first six years of his life back. I don't know if I can forgive Rene for that. Not fully. How do I trust them after that?"

"You trust them enough to share your home and raise your kid together," Pia points out. They stand back to assess the outline, then make a few alterations to exaggerate the victory pose.

"I guess." I examine the wall. Mo's going to love it once Pia finishes.

"No." Pia shakes their head at me. She gets out her paint and starts mixing the light blues and greens to block in Ollie's teal feathers. "Listen, you don't talk about anyone the way you talk about Rene. Not in all the years I've known you. So, it's obvious there's still something there. Don't give up that connection over an unfounded fear of getting hurt. I'm not saying you have to date them, or have sex or anything you aren't comfortable doing. I just think you should let them back into your life as a close friend. See what happens."

"I suppose," I say with a sigh. "There's Mo to consider if we blow up again, though."

"Sure. That's always possible. But don't you want to show Mo it's okay to take a chance on love? I almost missed out on being with Emil and Gregor because I was too scared of losing our friendship if things went south. I'm thankful every day that I gave our relationship a shot. They're my best friends and I can't imagine my life without them."

"It's not the same."

"No, I suppose it isn't," Pia concedes. "Just, don't close yourself off, Errol. If you don't want to be with Rene romantically, that's fine. I don't know what it's like to be demi, but I sort of get what it's like to have people assume love looks a certain way. So, you know, it's okay to love them in whatever way works for your family."

"Thanks," I say, meaning it. Pia's right. Rene and Mo are my family, and I love them. Both of them. That doesn't mean I'm *in* love with Rene anymore.

"And now that you're in the parent club, we'll have more excuses to get our families together," Pia winks at me. "Just think, in a few years Mo can babysit Rain for us."

The doorbell rings and I make my excuses to go let the new arrivals inside.

"Sure, scram. Maybe I'll be able to paint in peace, with

you out of my hair," Pia snarks at me with a teasing wink. I roll my eyes at them.

When I open the door Jude, Theo, Gui, and Paz crowd inside.

"We come bearing gifts," Theo proclaims as he brandishes a bakery box from Sin and Chocolate, the cafe where Paz works.

"You're going to be sad if you squash those," Jude observes.

"You'll cheer me back up," Theo waggles his eyebrows at his boyfriend, or fiancé now. That's still strange, Theo in a committed relationship. I roll my eyes.

"You can set the sweets on the counter with the other snack food," I instruct them. "Help yourselves to the fridge for drinks."

They grab refreshments and join Emil and Gregor in the living room. Mo is sitting with Emil, watching the influx of new people with wide eyes.

"Hey, little dude," Theo waves at Mo. "I'm Theo, he/him, and this is my boyfriend, Jude, also he/him. What's your name?"

"Mo. He/him. Hi," Mo sits on his hands and keeps shooting me nervous glances. I go to sit beside him. He climbs into my lap and pulls my arms around himself. The others introduce themselves and Mo gives them shy little waves.

"Hey, Momo, *tu vas bien?*" I murmur near his ear, just for him to hear.

Mo nods. "*Ouais,*" he breathes the word so low I almost miss it. My friends pretend not to notice he's turned shy.

"Want to break out the *Battle Fox*?" Theo suggests.

"*Je dis prems*… I mean dibs on Ollie," Mo declares, finding his voice now that there are video games on the table.

I smile into his dark hair and shoot Theo a grateful look for changing the focus. Theo and Gui get their consoles out, and Gregor grabs mine to set up so we can all connect in battle royale mode over my local area network.

"I made some chocolate brownies, if there are any little boys around who might like them," Paz mentions as we sort out controllers and teams.

"Can I?" Mo cranes his neck around to give me his very best 'no one ever feeds me' eyes.

"After we play. I don't want to get sticky goo on the controllers," I say, and that appeases him for now. I ignore Theo's amused snort at my word choice.

Once we divide into teams, Theo complains that they aren't fair, since he and Jude are on their own.

Mo pipes up, "Papa can play, right, Daddy?"

"If they want to, Momo, you can go ask them," I say, acutely aware that my buddies are all watching and curious to meet Rene.

"Come with me?" Mo asks.

"Yeah, of course." I set Mo on his feet and take his hand. We knock on the wall next to Rene's makeshift door. The flimsy partition hardly seems like adequate privacy. I should replace the slapdash temporary wall with something more sturdy if they're staying with me.

"Yeah?" Rene calls.

"Jouer avec nous, Papa!" Mo demands.

"Just a second, *mon chou,*" Rene says, there's some shuffling and then they open the curtain.

"Oh, hey, Errol. You alright with me joining the fun and games? I don't want to shoehorn myself into your day," Rene says, looking awkward as heck.

"The more the merrier," I say. "We need you to even up the teams, anyway. You live here, too. You don't have to hide in your room just because I invited people over."

"I wasn't sure..." Rene glances out at the crowded living room.

"These are my closest friends, they are going to want to meet my family, Rene."

I resist the urge to brush a stray lock of their hair back behind their ear. Our fragile renewed friendship isn't in a place to be exchanging casual touches. But I want my friends to meet Rene. Mo looks between us with an impatient stomp of his foot.

"Come on, we're going to miss the first match," he says.

"They'll wait on us, kiddo," I assure him, then for good measure I call to the others, "You're waiting for us to get back, right?"

"Sure, so long as you're bringing a teammate for Jude and I," Theo shoots back.

Gui gives him a shove. "Cool your jets, Theo."

Theo grumbles and rubs at his shoulder, playing as though the gentle push hurt him.

"*Jouons!*" Mo demands, and he tugs Rene and me both toward the living room.

"You sure this is okay?" Rene murmurs to me as we let our son drag us back to the party.

"Absolutely," I lie. Part of me fears this will go awry, that Rene won't like my friends or they won't like Rene. The folks I invited over today are the family I've built for myself since leaving home. But Rene and Mo are family, too. It'll suck if they don't all get along.

Mo doesn't let us stop until we're back in the living room. He announces, "This is my papa, Rene, they use they/them pronouns. Papa, sit so we can play."

The others all introduce themselves. Rene gives them awkward waves.

Once introductions are dealt with, Theo slaps a controller into Rene's hand. "Nice to meet you, Rene. You're on Jude and my team, so prepare to help us kick your kid's butt into next week. Gui, shove over so Rene can sit."

CHAPTER 8

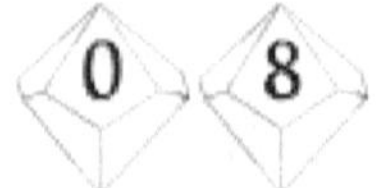

Rene

Errol's friends don't make me feel awkward about joining them. We don't kick Mo's butt. Mo, Errol, and Emil win the first game. We come in a close second. Theo insists on a rematch. We're about halfway through when the rest of the guests arrive. We pause for Errol to introduce Laura and Max to Mo and me.

The game allows up to four people to a team, so Errol and Laura go to see if Pia can join us for a few rounds. Theo wanders into the kitchen and grabs a brownie from a bakery box, helping himself to a plate and cutlery. He rummages in Errol's junk drawer and pulls out a stack of takeout menus.

"Score! Gotta love how organized Errol keeps stuff, what does everyone want for dinner?" he asks.

It's only four, so it seems early. Then again, there's twelve of us, thirteen counting the baby napping on the floor. Whatever we order will take a while to arrive. Jude joins Theo perusing the paper menus. The others pull out their phones to google the options. I sit awkwardly. My cell is a cheap prepaid flip phone. No data. No fancy bells and whistles. We've got my laptop and Mo's tablet for internet things. A fancy phone is an extravagance I couldn't justify on my meager budget.

Errol's friends all talk over each other as they debate food options. Errol and Pia emerge from Mo's room as the volume rises. Errol looks fondly exasperated with them.

"Children, please," he exclaims and they all subside. Then Errol takes charge, saying, "Why don't we pick a few places that way everyone gets what they want? There's enough of us to hit the free delivery minimums, regardless."

I watch him organize food for everyone with that familiar pang of regret. How different would life be if he'd been by my side to help me figure out my shit? No sense wondering. The answer is obvious, Errol has this adulting thing down better than I can dream of doing.

I jump on the sushi bandwagon with Emil and Pia. Emil makes a wistful comment about enjoying raw fish while he can and hoping that it will be the last time for a while. I blink at the cryptic words and the way his partners give him reassuring touches.

"We're doing IVF," Pia explains in an undertone when she catches my curious expression. They shrug and gesture toward Emil. "He wanted a turn carrying the next kid."

"Ah. Gotcha, I hope it works out for you," I say, trying not to glance at the napping baby who can't be a year old yet. I can't even imagine wanting another infant when Mo was that tiny. But their family plans are none of my business.

"Thanks. Me too," Emil agrees in a tight voice.

"Think you and Errol might want another?" Pia asks with a mischievous glint in their eyes.

"Hell, no," I say, more emphatically than necessary. Emil frowns and shrinks in like the words sting, so I elaborate, "We aren't together. Mo's destined to remain an only child, much to his displeasure."

"Must've been rough, having him on your own," Pia says, her expression full of empathy.

"I got Mo out of it, so… " I shrug off just how rough it got. I glimpse the kid in question hanging off of Theo. Mo is shit-talking about how he's going to beat Theo in the next round of *Battle Fox*. Theo dangles him upside down and demands that he admit Ollie Owl is about to face an epic beat-down. Mo's giggles show no signs of stopping, and Theo seems practiced at roughhousing with the kid, not like he might drop Mo or anything. Errol mentioned he has a nephew, so I just monitor them, happy that Mo seems happy.

"He seems like a great kid," Pia says, interrupting my train of thought.

"Thanks, I like to think so," I agree, then I change the subject, "So, what's everyone getting?"

"Did you want to pick a bunch of rolls to share, or each get our own?" Emil asks.

"I'm up for sharing," Pia glances to me, "Rene, want in on that?"

"Sure, any dietary restrictions?" I agree.

"No shellfish for me," Emil says.

"Allergies?" I ask, because if so, that could be serious. I had a teammate with a peanut allergy, and I had to be careful about Mo having PB & Js if she was going to be around him.

"Not kosher," Emil clarifies.

"Ah. Ok. Is the rest of it kosher?" I have zero clue what religious dietary restrictions mean for him, beyond no bacon. At least, I think it means no bacon.

"Eh, depends on if the restaurant gets certified. I'm not actually observant, I sort of just follow the broad strokes," Emil admits.

We select an excessive number of rolls and Emil throws in a few orders of sashimi too. I'm second guessing the sharing thing when I take in the price tally. Split three ways, it's still going to be a ton.

"Um, we might have gone a touch overboard," I suggest.

"I like variety," Emil says sheepishly. "I'm the one who picked most of the expensive rolls, though. So, like, if you want to just chip in fifteen, Pia and I will cover the rest."

I hesitate. I don't want charity, and I don't want to make a bad impression with Errol's friends. On the other hand, Mo needs new school clothes, and I still haven't figured out daycare. The more I search, the more it appears I'll need to sell a kidney to get him a full-time spot for the last few weeks of summer. Let alone pay for it.

Pia nudges me. "It's fine, Emil likes all the fancy artistic rolls. We've got it covered."

"If you're sure," I hedge, but I dig the money out of my wallet. Pia takes the cash. It's still more than I should spend, but everyone else already has their orders placed. Backing out doesn't feel like an option.

Emil gives me a radiant smile. "We're sure."

"Yeah, this place makes fun rolls. And Errol is a loser who never invites us over," Pia says loud enough for Errol to hear. He flips her the bird after checking that Mo still has his attention focused on using Theo as a jungle gym.

"I invite you, but no one ever wants to venture so far into the burbs for their weekend fun. You all live closer to downtown," Errol argues.

"Yeah, well, you've got the biggest place, we should gather here more often," Gui suggests.

"You just don't want to host because the mess makes Paz too grumpy to put out—" Theo teases. A sharp throat clearing sound from Errol and an elbow jab followed by a pointed glance at Mo from Jude makes Theo tack on a hasty, "—the trash. Paz hates to put out the trash after a big party."

"Nice save," Errol says, the words exuding dry sarcasm. "Seriously, dude, watch your mouth with the dirty language around my kid."

"What did he say?" Mo asks with a confused frown. "Trash is dirty, but it's not a curse word."

"Yeah, I'm working on it," Theo grimaces, "Erin read me the riot act the last time I watched Sky. She didn't like him saying—"

Jude clears his throat and elbows Theo again.

"What? Mo's old enough to say, 'suck it, loser,' isn't he?" Theo ruffles Monet's hair and sets him on his feet.

Mo giggles and tries to get Theo to swing him in the air some more. "Suck it, loser. Swing me up!"

"Nope, he really isn't," I interject, leveling the kid with a 'watch it' look until he apologizes and asks Theo to play more politely. I intervene more because he'll get in trouble for words like that at school than because I care about curbing his language. And I still have to figure out his school registration on top of the daycare thing.

Shit, I'm going to have a busy week before my new job starts. I should spend this weekend time while Mo has fun with his other dad to get a jump start on that. Otherwise I'm going to be relying on *Battle Fox* to keep the kid busy while I research our options and make phone calls. Not that there will be staff answering the phones in the offices I need to call on a Saturday afternoon during summer vacation.

Besides, Pia already placed our food order and the others are putting away their phones before reclaiming their game controllers. Looks like we're going to play another round while we wait on food delivery. This time Mo teams up with Jude, Theo, and Max. I'm on a team with Paz, Gui, and Errol.

Errol tries to organize us to victory, calling out orders to work as a team. We still lose, but I can't help the warmth spreading through my chest when he offers me praise. High-fiving me after a move that knocks Laura's character off the stage just before she can send Ollie Owl flying.

The casual affection when he ruffles my hair and says we'll get them next time as I'm knocked out of the competition fills me with nostalgia. I miss the lazy childhood weekends when playing video games with Errol seemed like the most important thing in my world, with hockey coming in a close second. For a few hours, I let myself have that again, like a familiar old blanket soothing away my worries.

After the games, Mo breaks out his brightly colored nail polish collection, a holdover from one of my many failed attempts to quit chewing on my nails. I warn Errol's friends to avoid the clear coat, since it has a bittering agent in it. Mo prefers bright colors and sparkles, so his collection is pretty vibrant. Just because I gave up on having nice nails doesn't mean Mo has to follow suit.

The kid has a good time doing everyone's nails before they leave. They're all good sports about it. Theo preens like a peacock over finding a shade of hot pink that matches his current hair color. Max lets Mo pick his colors, and he ends up with rainbow stripes with a glittery top coat.

It's fun to see Mo getting along and laughing with the people in Errol's life. They truly seem happy to welcome Mo into their little family. Errol built the life he said he wanted here. After tonight, I'm hopeful that maybe there's room for me in it, too.

CHAPTER 9

0 9

Errol

After our late night with my buddies, Rene, Mo, and I spend a lazy Sunday vegging out to old Star Trek episodes as a family. We let Mo stay up past his bedtime to watch Pia work on his wall, and then he crashed with Rene on the guest futon to avoid the fumes from the drying paint, so he's sleepy over brunch.

Mo didn't get to send Laurent pictures of the finished Ollie art, since it was late by the time everyone left last night. The two of them have a video chat after we eat. Mo shows off his wall mural and his freshly painted smiley face nails. Their conversation devolves into playing around with video filters until Laurent's parents call an end to his screen time.

While Mo is occupied, Rene and I get some time to catch up. Our Saturday spent gaming together changed something between us. Like it flipped a switch back to old times with Rene—my best friend, not the ex who broke my heart and lied to me. I loved Rene as a friend before anything romantic or sexual developed between us, and as we chat I can't deny I still love them that way, even after all these years.

I didn't expect to feel a lingering attraction to them when they returned, but it's there, worn thin by the emotional distance between us after years of no contact. The more time I spend with them, the more that old emotional connection rekindles, along with all my complex feelings toward Rene. Is it easier to fall in love the second time? It seems to be. Or maybe it's easier to love someone who loves my son, who laughs at the same silly jokes as him. We've got so much shared history, it's hard to say if this is just nostalgia, or the start of something more.

All I know is, the more time I spend with my little family, the more I want to reclaim everything I used to have in common with Rene. All our in-jokes and remember whens. The stolen moments and ill-advised pranks. The partner who pushed me to be more spontaneous and who followed my lead when situations got sticky. The dreams we shared of a future that isn't quite what we've built after our paths diverged, but bears a striking resemblance to the major strokes. I'm making a living in the arts and Rene gets to be on the ice as part of their job. Our teenage selves couldn't have asked for much more than that.

The second week of living with Rene and Mo is much like the first, except it feels less like we're acting like a family, and more like we're becoming one. When Mo calls me Daddy, it sounds less forced. When he hugs me at bedtime or high fives me after a game it seems more heartfelt.

Each day, we eat breakfast and dinner as a family. All of

us watch a show, play a game, or work on an activity together before putting Mo to bed, and then Rene and I tidy up together. When the house is set to rights, we relax in the living room before bed.

For the first week, I retired to my room to work on commissions at my desk, like usual. But this week I've been watching Rene's baking show with them while I do rough preliminary sketches to unwind. It's not as ergonomic as working at my desk, and I couldn't do the final pieces with Rene's feet on my lap, jostling me whenever the bakers on TV make something particularly tasty looking, but I like the sense of companionship from just sitting with them and sharing space.

Thursday morning dawns much like the rest of the week. I find Mo and Rene chattering over breakfast when I exit my room, ready for work. Mo switches from French to English when he catches sight of me. Rene hands me a plate of eggs and toast and a mug of coffee.

It's nice to share a meal before leaving for work instead of scarfing down toast at the office. Work provides the toast, at least. Too bad everyone has burning questions and impromptu meetings first thing, by the time I get around to eating it, the toast is often cold and unappetizing. This is better.

Rene beams at me, bright enough to make my breath catch when I compliment their cooking. Their kitchen skills are still basic. At least they've improved from forgetting to add water and starting a fire in the microwave while trying to make easy-mac when we were teens. Good thing, too, or poor Mo would live on nuked hotdogs. That used to be the only meal in Rene's repertoire outside of PB & Js. There's the familiar pang of thinking about all the family meals I wasn't around for. I have to stop torturing myself with this shit.

"Are you getting excited to start work next week?" I ask Rene. They've said little about the new job, and I'm curious.

"Oh, uh, yeah," Rene nods, then bites their lip.

"What's wrong?" I ask, frowning.

"It's nothing." Rene cuts their eyes to Mo and shakes their head, mouthing, 'later.'

My frown deepens, but I make a mental note to ask about it again. Mo finishes his cereal and asks if he can play on the Switch.

"No, buddy," Rene says, tone brooking no argument. "Play with your toys for a bit, or read a book, screen time later."

"Ah, man, do I gotta wait, Daddy?" Mo turns his big soulful eyes and pouty face toward me, sensing I'm the parent most likely to cave on the rules.

"Yes, you do," Rene insists.

"Listen to your papa, and put your dish in the dishwasher before you go," I say. Hell, if I'm letting him think he can play us against each other, even if I don't particularly care when he uses his screen time. Mo sulks as he takes care of his bowl, then stomps to his room. He stops short of slamming his door. Rene gives me an amused look.

"Kids," they say, with fond exasperation. Then they explain, "I need to make some calls later today, and it will be easier if he's distracted with the Switch."

"Ah, that makes sense. Work stuff?"

"Sort of." Rene shifts in their seat and glances at the ancient laptop on our coffee table. "So, you asked what's wrong, I need to find someone to watch Mo while I'm working and I'm coming up blank. Plus, the school may or may not have a slot for him in the French immersion track. They want him to do a language assessment for him to get priority, and we need his records from last year. Too bad I keep missing the secretary at his old elementary school."

"Wow. Okay, that's a lot. Why didn't you mention anything sooner?" I ask.

Rene sighs. "Truth? I'm not used to sharing responsibility for him. I can handle it. Everything is just different here, you know? You'd think we moved to another country, not a different province," Rene says with a rueful chuckle.

"You'd think it would be similar," I agree.

"Similar, but enough of a difference to trip me up. Like, for example, there we had a single daycare waiting list everyone could use. Here it's all piecemeal and the fees are... much higher. It was a big change when I moved there, too. I wasn't sure if it was really that different, or a factor of being an adult with adult responsibilities dumped on my head."

Rene hunches in on themself, looking so vulnerable it makes my heart ache for them.

"Come here." I open my arms and Rene leans into me, letting me hug them as I say, "We'll figure this out together. It might be different, but you aren't alone."

"I'm not sure moving back was such a great idea," they murmur, chilling me. There's no way I'm letting them walk back out of my life without a fight. I squeeze Rene tight.

"It was. The best idea. You focus on getting Mo registered for school, since you seem to have all the information and his old school knows you. It sounds like that's enough on your plate for now. I'll figure out the daycare situation for the summer."

"He'll need after school care, too," Rene mumbles against my shoulder.

"We've got time to figure that out," I say.

Rene barks a laugh. "You'd think that. There are only so many available slots, the best rated programs fill up fast. We're already behind schedule, with moving over the summer. Ask your friends with the baby. I'll bet you they're already looking at preschool waiting lists for the kid they're still trying to conceive."

That gives me the perfect idea, I kiss the top of Rene's head without thinking about it. The sort of casual affection I never had to think about twice with them, before. They stiffen in my arms and I move away, rubbing sheepishly at the back of my neck.

"Sorry, old habits. Um. Speaking of Emil, though, he mentioned something about wanting to start his own daycare. I bet if we offered to pay him, he'd watch Mo for us."

"Yeah?" Rene bites their nails, sounding uncertain. "Are you sure that's a good idea?"

"Emil used to teach pre-K. He's got a degree in early childhood education. He adores working with little ones. Mo seemed to like him on Saturday. They chatted while Pia finished the painting after the *Battle Fox* tournament ended. We can ask him if it's an option, anyway."

Rene studies my face, then nods. "Yeah, okay, talk to Emil about it. Pass along my number? Sorry to be flaky about this. I worry about him."

"If you aren't comfortable asking my friends to watch Mo, we can consider other options. Like I said, I'll look into it. Worst-case scenario, I can try to take some time off next week or get my mom to come watch him during the week until we get him in somewhere or school starts."

"Oh, shit, we still have to introduce him to your folks, huh?" Rene's eyes widen and they go back to chewing on their nails.

"Yeah. We do," I say, gently taking their hand and squeezing before they hurt themself with the nervous habit.

"They're going to hate me," Rene wails.

"I can't promise they won't get upset about not knowing sooner, but they won't hate you. If they want to know their grandson, they're going to have to forgive and forget. Whatever issues anyone has with the choices you made, it's obvious you did the best you could for Mo. I won't let anyone badmouth you in front of him, okay?"

"Thanks." Rene swallows hard. "That means a lot. I... just, thanks, Errol. You've been so understanding and I—"

"Hush, we're a team, okay? I have to get to work. I'll text Emil about getting in touch with you and research other daycare options in case he can't do it. We can figure out the grandparent thing once you've settled into your new job."

"Okay." Rene nods, collecting themself. "Sounds good. Have a good day at work."

"Thanks," I grin and resist the urge to touch them. This feels like the moment I'd lean in and peck them on the cheek, if we were a couple. Then we'd exchange a flippant 'I love you' before I walked out the door. Instead, I stare at them just a little too long for comfort. Then I take care of my dirty dishes and poke my head into Mo's room to give him a goodbye hug.

As I let myself out the door, Rene is watching me from the kitchen, a hungry intensity in their gaze as they wave and call out another goodbye.

CHAPTER 10

1 0

Rene

I spend the day Thursday getting my shit together for Mo's school registration stuff. I finally get in touch with Mo's old school and they agree to fax his records to the new school. Then I schedule an appointment for us to meet with the administrators tomorrow for a tour and in person meeting.

By the time that's all handled, Mo's used up all his screen time. He's bouncing off the walls from the sugary granola bars I fed him to tide him over until I can put together a real lunch for us.

"Let's go for a walk to the park, eh?" I suggest with more enthusiasm than I feel.

Mo makes a face. "*J'ai faim.*"

"*Nous pouvons acheter des sandwiches,*" I wheedle him with the promise of restaurant food. Mo brightens. I know my cooking isn't the greatest, so I try not to act offended that he'd rather eat even a sandwich someone else made.

"*Est-ce une promesse*?" Mo asks.

"Yes, I promise. We'll buy them on the way and eat at the park. Like a picnic," I agree. Then I wince and open a tab on my laptop to check if there's enough money on my debit card to keep that promise. There is. Barely. If they cost too much, we can buy one to share. Mo gives me one of his looks, like he sees right through my false cheer. It will be okay, Errol isn't charging me for food or rent and I'll be getting my first paycheck soon. "Get your shoes on, *mon chou*."

Mo goes to get ready. I grab his backpack and stuff it with our reusable water bottles, a couple of apples, and a handful of granola bars. I hesitate before adding a big bag of chips, too. That isn't something we bought on our last grocery run. Hopefully Errol won't mind sharing. Mo's got his shoes on and is waiting by the door by the time I gather my phone, wallet, the house keys, and our lunch stuff.

We wander in the general direction where I remember having seen a park. To distract Mo from the fact I'm unsure of where we're going, or how far it is, we play a game. I have him count all the white cars he sees along the way. I pick blue cars and he seems content to count as we go. We happen past a donair place, perfect for my budget. If we don't get any sides, I can afford to get us each a pita. Mo wrinkles his nose at the hummus and garlic sauce, so I get him just plain chicken on his pita. Light on the cabbage and bright purple turnips. I get mine all dressed.

As I pay, I ask the cashier about the closest park. The question earns me an expression like I'm mental for asking until I lie and explain my phone died. The person pulls up a map app on their sleek device to show me how to get where we're going. I thank them and add the pitas to our bag of lunch supplies.

Mo gives me another of his long looks, but he doesn't comment other than to remind me he is kicking my ass at the car counting game. I admonish him not to say ass. He mutters that Daddy's friends said it, so why can't he. I pretend not to hear his grumbling. Got to choose my battles. We make it to the park and eat our lunch without incident.

Mo runs off to play on the playground equipment and I settle in to watch him and enjoy the sunny weather. My phone buzzes in my pocket.

"Allo?" I say, old habit kicking in.

"Hey, Rene. This is Emil. Errol gave me your number."

"Oh, yeah, hi. How's it going?" I ask, shifting my phone to the other ear and trying to relax.

"Oh, you know, dealing with a teething baby. Rain's napping in their swing, so I figured I'd take advantage of the silence to call you."

"Oh, wow, you're brave to speak of the silence," I joke. "Haven't you learned not to jinx it yet?"

Emil chuckles. "So you're superstitious, huh? I figure they'll be down for at least an hour, I just gave them some Tylenol for the pain, and that seems to help."

"That's good. I remember those days, hang in there." I wince because I took that part of parenting away from Errol. Why does everything have to remind me of my screwups? "Did Errol, uh, mention what he was thinking?"

"He asked how I'd feel about watching Mo for you guys over the summer."

"Not a guy," I correct him, bracing for a reaction. It's the sort of throwaway thing that will continue to grate on my nerves if I don't say anything. I don't have the energy for this conversation, if he pushes back. I'm also not ready to let it pass and then have to hear him say it over and over.

"My bad, thanks for telling me. I can watch Mo for you two. I'm home with Rain, anyway. If Errol can drop him off and pick him up on his commute that should be fine, he works similar hours to Pia, right?"

"Yeah, I think so."

"Great, we can work out the exact details once you and Errol talk things over. He mentioned you weren't sure about liability and stuff. I have an early education certification, and I'm up to date on my pediatric first aid certs, too. I'm looking into getting licensed as an in-home daycare provider, if that would ease your mind?"

"It would."

"Great, well, I'm working on the paperwork to make things official but I can watch Mo next week. As a family friend or babysitter or whatever, if you're comfortable with it. The only tiny issue is that I have appointments with the fertility specialist. Gregor and Pia have been taking time off to watch Rain while I'm busy. I should still be able to take him those days. Heck, for the labs I've been having Pia take Rain during her lunch, so I can bring Mo by the studio to eat with his other dad those days. If not, I'll try to give you enough notice to find another sitter for the day."

"That's fine. Would Mo and I be able to visit your place before we do this?"

"Sure, you can swing by this afternoon, or tomorrow, if that's easier?"

"We're at the park, now. So tomorrow might work better. Although, shoot, we've got meetings for his school stuff. Hmm."

"I can text you the address. Or if you hop on the Sky-Train at the station near Errol's place and take it to the Granville street stop, I can meet you there. I need to walk Otis once the goober is awake, anyway."

"Yeah, okay. Otis?"

"Our dog. He's a big softie, great with kids. Is that alright?"

"It's fine, except now you're going to have Mo begging me for a dog and a baby sibling," I joke. Emil laughs.

"Can't help you with that. We can hope he gets his playing with babies and puppies fix at my place. You and Errol can encourage him to enjoy being a pampered only child at home."

"There's an idea. Great, well, I'm going to let him run off some energy before we head over, and give your little one time to finish their nap."

"Sounds good. Text when you're getting on the train and we should be able to get there around the same time you arrive."

"Will do. Thanks, Emil."

"No problem. Mo's sweet, and having him around during the day will get my butt in gear about filing the paperwork. This is a win-win. I'll pick up some age-appropriate toys and activities for him, but this will be fun, text me."

"I will. See you soon." I hang up, feeling less wary of the plan. Emil sounds genuinely interested in watching Mo. Like this isn't Errol's friend offering us charity. We'll pay him for his services and he'll be building a business he seems invested in. Win-win, like he said. Plus, I like Emil from the few interactions we've had. He didn't so much as blink about me carrying Mo. Granted, he's also trans, but it's still nice. Not having that awkward moment of people questioning how Errol and I made a kid. No one demanding I justify my identity just because I chose to use the parts I was born with.

Mo seems to enjoy the playground, so I let him play until the pair of siblings he's digging in the dirt with have to leave. He wanders over to me once they're gone. I get him cleaned up. Baby wipes: not just for babies. Then I hand him a granola bar and we follow the signs directing us across the park to the SkyTrain station.

I text Emil before we pay the fare. I wince at the cost, it's not too steep, but every penny counts until my new job starts. Too bad this is the only way we're getting downtown without Errol's car, so I just have to suck it up. If we hang out until Errol leaves work, we can catch a ride home with him to save the cost of a return trip.

I text Errol after we grab two seats near the door. The SkyTrain into downtown isn't crowded at this hour, not like it will be if we head back out to Burnaby during the evening commute.

Rene: Visiting Emil with Mo. Can we bum a ride home tonight?

Errol: Yeah, I'll give Pia a ride and meet you two at their place.

Rene: Cool.

Errol: You and Mo have dinner plans?

Rene: No, why?

Errol: I need a reason to take my family out for dinner?

Rene: You don't have to go to any trouble.

Errol: I want to. You deserve a break from cooking, anyway.

Rene: I see how it is, you just want to avoid eating my food. You're conspiring with Mo, aren't you?

Errol: I would never! ;) I should get back to work, meet you at Pia's around six. Give Mo a hug for me.

Rene: Will do.

"Are you talking to Daddy, Papa?" Mo is watching me when I put my phone away.

"Yeah, how did you know?" I ask him.

"You smile a lot when you talk to him."

"I guess I do," I agree, ruffling the kid's hair.

"Does that mean you might change your minds about sharing a room and getting me a baby sibling?" Mo asks, swinging his legs in front of his seat.

"Oh, Momo. No. Papa isn't having any more kids. We've talked about this," I remind him.

"Okay. But, we could adopt one."

"That's not as easy as you might think, bud."

"Can we at least get a dog?" Mo suggests.

"Your daddy and I will have to discuss that one." I say, leaving wiggle room that Mo will doubtless make me regret.

"Mhm," Mo hums in agreement. Just when I think he's done asking questions, he says, "Are you and Daddy going to be a couple again?"

"Does that matter?" I ask, the question stings, salt in a raw wound of my own making.

"No. I guess not. Except Daddy makes you smile and I like it when you smile, Papa."

Ouch, my heart. "I'm just happy you have your daddy in your life, Momo. You're a good kid, you know?"

"I know." Mo shoots me his gap-toothed grin, and my heart melts all over again. This kid makes me putty in his hands. "Where are we going?"

"To visit Emil and baby Rain and help them walk their dog, Otis." I say.

"Oh, okay. You think I can play with Otis?"

"Probably."

"Cool. I can practice for when we get a dog."

I let that go instead of reminding him I never agreed to a pet. "How would you like to stay with Emil, Rain, and Otis during the day while Papa works?"

"Do they have toys?" he asks, eyes narrowing.

"I'm not sure, but you can bring some of your things if they don't."

"Then that sounds okay."

"Good."

"Will Pia paint me more Ollie Owls?" Mo asks idly.

"You can always ask."

That seems to satisfy his curiosity, Mo turns to stare out the window at the passing city-scape until we get to the underground parts of the route. When we emerge from the metro station at street level, Emil is easy to spot with a baby strapped to his chest and a large dog on a leash. Otis licks Mo, making him giggle.

Emil greets my kid like they've been friends forever, crouching down on his level to introduce him to the dog. The last of my reservations melt away as I watch Mo grin and chatter with Emil with none of his usual shyness around strangers. He bonded with Errol's friends at their video game day. Mo seems comfortable with Emil, and Errol knows the guy well enough to call him a close friend. This will be okay.

CHAPTER 11

Errol

I walk Pia inside after parking near their place, since I need to discuss the details of our childcare arrangement with Emil. He's feeding Rain a bottle as we walk inside, Mo and Rene are sitting with him.

We greet them after taking off our shoes by the door. Pia kisses Emil and Rain and I muss Mo's hair and wave to Rene.

"How was your day, sweetheart?" Pia asks Emil.

"We're good, hashing out daycare deets with Rene. Mo is quite the big helper," Emil replies. "Only need to finalize a few things with Errol and sign the paperwork."

"Sounds great, I just need to borrow him in the kitchen for a minute first," Pia says, then she drags me with her to the kitchen, where she gets out ingredients to cook dinner.

"What's up?" I ask, knowing they didn't drag me away to help in the kitchen.

"Nothing. Well, except the cooking wine I need for the

sauce, you'd think three short people would stop using the top shelf, but there you go, mind reaching it for me?" Pia points to the cabinet and I get down the wine with a pointed glance at the step stool folded up in the corner.

"Anything else you need to exploit my height for?" I ask dryly.

"Not at the moment. So, how are things with you and Rene since our chat on Saturday. I'm making veggie lasagna, there should be enough for everyone, if you three want to stay?" they offer.

"We're good. Can we get a rain check on dinner? I promised to take Mo and Rene out to eat tonight," I decline the invite.

"Oh, well, in that case, we can keep Mo for you, if you want to woo your person," Pia suggests in a conspiratorial undertone. "Give you both a break from kid duty."

For a second, I consider it. I could take Rene on a date. Get reacquainted. Treat them to a nice meal. We never got to do that stuff when we dated as teens.

Our friendship shifted to include sexual stuff when I'd admitted to wanting to kiss Rene after picking them up from their hockey practice one day. They'd leaned across the console and pressed our lips together. It didn't fundamentally change our relationship much. We already spent every spare moment together before dating, the whole town knew Rene and Errol were attached at the hip.

We were kids and dating meant playing video games together, and dry humping on the couch in my parents' basement. Every so often, we mixed it up with make out sessions in the back row of the movie theatre. Or accidentally making a kid in my ramshackle tree fort because we were too horny to go buy condoms. We were monogamous and Rene's cycles were irregular enough that we figured it would be okay, just the once.

So, yeah, it would be nice to take Rene on a real date. I shake my head at my own foolishness. Rene and I aren't dating. Taking them out for dinner is asking to stir up more memories and relive old feelings that are better left buried. If we go there, it seems inevitable that I'm going to keep falling for Rene all over again and the more I care, the more my old attraction seems to bubble to the surface.

"Thanks for the offer, but I'm not sure that's the best idea."

"Suit yourself," Pia says with a shrug. "Doesn't have to be a date. You two could just enjoy some kid-free time. In my experience, sometimes it's nice to take off the parent hat and just be an adult for an evening. I wonder when Rene last got a night out to relax?"

I scowl at Pia and she gives me her best innocent eyes and a wink. That wink says they know they've shamed me into going along with their absurd matchmaking plans. Subtle, Pia is not, but she's right about giving Rene a kid-free night to decompress.

I can accomplish that goal by watching Mo solo for the evening. I haven't gotten to do that yet, but it's bound to happen eventually. Might as well be tonight. I can handle being alone with my kid. But other than my friends, whom they've met once, I'm the only person Rene knows in the city.

Besides, it hasn't escaped my notice that they're barely getting by. No one who can afford better still uses an old flip phone. And I caught them doing the mental math about whether they could spare the cash for takeout with my buddies over the weekend. If I tell them to get lost for the evening, it won't send the message that I want to give them a break. Rene is still so insecure about their place in my home and the little family we're cobbling together that I'm sure they'd see it as a rejection.

I glance over to where Mo sits brushing the big furry dog on the living room floor. Rene and Emil occupy the couch, chatting while Emil feeds Rain.

"I'll see what Rene thinks," I say. Then I leave Pia humming to themself as they prep their dinner ingredients.

"Hey, stud, Pia all set?" Rene greets me with a wan smile as I approach. I can picture the version of reality where I sit beside them on the couch, drape an arm around them and greet them with a quick kiss.

Instead, I plop down beside Mo and Otis. "Hey, Rene. Yep, they just needed me to get down the wine for their sauce. How was your day, Momo?"

"Good. Papa got us pitas, and we had a picnic at the park. Then I got to play with baby Rain and Emil let me walk Otis. I'm going to help him so I can learn how to take care of our dog."

"Oh, are we getting a dog now?" I tease, ruffling the kid's hair. Mo scowls and tries to fix his hair.

"Not now," he says, in his best 'duh' voice, "for my birthday."

I raise a brow at Rene, doubting they'd have made that sort of promise without discussing it with me. Not considering how timid they've been about so much as buying a different brand of toilet paper for our place.

"I said Daddy and I would talk about maybe getting a dog at some point, Mo. I never agreed to getting you a dog for your birthday." Rene corrects.

"Please?" Mo breaks out the pouty face.

"We'll discuss it, bud, that's the best you're getting out

of me," Rene says. Mo looks ready to protest, but Emil steps in to defuse the situation.

"In the meantime, you and Otis are going to be best buds, okay?" Emil offers. "Why don't you go ask Pia for a treat to give to Otis while I have a quick chat with your folks?"

"Okay," Mo sets aside the brush and goes to the kitchen, Otis following on his heels, already tuned into the kid being a fount of treats and attention.

"So, are we set for me to watch him starting next week?" Emil asks, looking between Rene and me.

"What do you say, Rene?" I ask, knowing they had reservations about the idea.

"Yeah. I think that will work." Rene smiles.

"Great!" Emil nods decisively. He asks me about exact hours. Since I drive by here on my daily commute, anyway, I'll be handling most of the pickup and drop-off duties. We go back and forth hammering out the details. Then Emil has us fill out the paperwork to formalize our agreement and give him permission to give our kid Tylenol, sunscreen, or anything else he needs.

"Pia invited Mo to stay for dinner so Rene and I can go out, if that's alright?" I mention once we have everything arranged.

"Are you and Papa having a date?" Mo pipes up to ask. He gazes between us with big hopeful eyes.

"We're just going out as friends, Momo," Rene corrects him.

"Oh. Okay. Have fun. Can I feed Otis his dinner and take him for another walk, Emil?" Mo loses interest in us in favor of getting his fill of the dog.

"Sure," Emil says to Mo. Then he turns to us and says, "We've got Mo, have fun and take your time. This tiny one has been a fussasaurus with their new teeth coming in. So I expect I'll be up late, anyway," Emil baby-talks the last few sentences at Rain, who is squirming and making disgruntled noises.

"We won't be too late," Rene assures him. We say our goodbyes to Mo while he's distracted playing with Otis, then leave. On an impulse, I grab Rene's hand as we exit the building. They seem surprised before relaxing into letting me hold their hand.

"This okay?" I ask.

"Yeah. Not used to it," they reply, swinging our joined hands.

"What sort of food would you want?" I ask, glancing up and down the street. Pia's place is downtown on the west side, so there are several restaurants within a short walk. No need to give up the primo metered parking spot I found a half a block away. With my free hand, I open the app on my phone to extend my parking for a couple hours.

"I'm not picky," they say, and then wince. "Someplace cheap, please?"

"I invited you to dinner, I'm paying," I insist.

"That was when it was Mo, too," Rene argues.

"Nope." I shake my head. "This is my treat. Once you get paid, you can fight with me about splitting the bill. But I figure I owe you about six years of back payment on child support."

"No," Rene says flatly. They drop my hand and stop in their tracks, shaking their head with vehemence. "Absolutely not! I didn't reenter your life to get money out of you, Errol. You don't owe me anything for taking care of *our* son. Not when you didn't know he existed." The horrified guilt on Rene's face convinces me to drop the subject. It's a complicated situation, but the bottom line is, it's obvious Rene gave up a lot to take care of Mo. All so I could build a stable life and career without them in it. I might wish they'd told me sooner, but right or wrong, I now have the means to make things easier for both Mo and Rene. Hell if I'm letting anything stop me from doing just that.

"Tell me what you want for dinner, Rene," I ask again.

"Emil told me about a Mexican place close by. I guess the three of them go there for date nights. Their tacos sound tasty," Rene suggests.

"And the fact Emil raves about their half-price tacos and margaritas on Tuesdays and Thursdays has nothing to do with your decision?" I ask, amused at their reticence to ask for something more extravagant. I'd give it to them, and they seem to understand that.

Rene looks abashed as they ask, "Don't you like tacos?"

"I do. You never used to, though." I say.

Rene shrugs. "Tastes change, Errol. Besides, I still like tequila just fine." They wink at me.

"Mexican it is, then!" I declare. I know the way to the restaurant, so I turn in the correct direction.

"Can't wait," Rene says. There's a hint of heat in their expression. Heat that reminds me just how much they enjoyed our previous adventures with tequila.

Rene is a handsy, horny drunk. Or at least, they had been in high school. I have vivid memories of the first time we drank together. I swiped a bottle of tequila from my folks after a family BBQ when I was seventeen and Rene was sixteen. My aunt liked to make pitchers of margaritas, but my parents never drank the stuff, so I figured they wouldn't miss it.

They hadn't, but they sure noticed Rene drunk off

their ass stumbling up the stairs when I tried to sneak them into my room after midnight. We'd fooled around in our tree fort and then fallen asleep. Woke up in the wee hours freezing cold, still buzzed out of our skulls, and needing the washroom. That night after our overindulgence, I knew Rene would have gotten in serious trouble with their folks. So, I snuck them into my room, wasted.

I got grounded for a month. Not for drinking. For lying, sneaking around, and putting Rene into a compromising position. Rene's folks would have flipped if they knew about that night. They already didn't like us dating. Rene's friend and teammate, Caro, had provided cover for us, corroborating made up sleepovers more times than I could count.

My folks were realists about sex, they figured I'd be doing it once I started dating. They bought me condoms and told me to use them, no matter the gender of the person I was with. Awkward as heck, considering I'd yet to experience any sort of sexual attraction at the time. But once Rene and I started fooling around, I'd listened to their advice. Most of the time.

Except the one stupid night over spring break, when I brought tequila home from school with me for my visit. A choice driven by fond memories of that first night. We limited ourselves to just enough to get buzzed during that fateful second adventure with tequila.

Now that I know how much that night changed our lives, I can't help wondering if we might still be together if not for that series of reckless choices. The drinking and fucking even though our stashed box of condoms turned out to be empty. Then it hits me that if not for that night, Mo wouldn't exist. I can't bring myself to wish for that reality, no matter how much it hurt to lose Rene.

"Earth to Errol, where did you go?" Rene waves a hand in front of my face. Their brow furrows with concern as they press the back of one hand to my forehead. It's such a parental gesture of checking that I'm okay, I can't help a low chuckle. "I'm right here, just reminiscing."

"About our epic first BJ?" Rene asks, a twinkle in their eyes.

"Yeah," I say. It was a memorable night, even if parts of it were less than ideal.

"Well, you know, we could always stage a reenactment, for old times' sake," Rene jokes.

"I don't think I need a repeat of you puking jizz and tequila on my shoes, but thanks, anyway," I say.

"Shit, did I really do that?" Rene asks.

"Yeah, on the way back to my folks' place, not surprised you don't remember. You got totally blitzed," I say. I'd been little better off, but it had been pretty gross, so that detail stood out in my memories.

"Well, I'm surprised you wanted to date me after that."

I scoff. "Rene, I don't think there's anything you could have done back then to get me to want to stop dating you."

"Except get knocked up, fuck off across the country to hide it, and publically hit you hard in your weak spots to keep you from coming after me?" Rene asks. There's a bitter edge of self-mockery in their tone.

I reach for them, swallowing hard. Because, yeah, all that had hurt. Yet I still yearn to declare, 'no, not even that.' Not even hiding Mo from me for the next six years could make me stop loving Rene.

"Do you think we'd still be together, if you hadn't run?" I ask instead of making reckless declarations neither of us are ready to handle.

Rene shrugs. "No one stays in love with their first crush forever, stud."

"Not no one," I protest.

"Very few people marry their high school sweetheart, and even fewer stay with them, Errol. The odds were always against us and throwing a kid in the mix on top of being young and stupid?" They shake their head, regret clear.

"I wish I'd had all the facts. I wish I thought to question why you said what you did."

"Why didn't you?" Rene asks.

"I was hurt, mostly. And part of me wondered if you hadn't just been using being with me as an escape from your family. When my folks let you stay over, it meant you could be yourself under their roof. And then after graduation, you didn't need that escape anymore. You didn't need me." That part had hurt the most, feeling used and discarded.

"No." Rene lays a hand on my bicep. "Never that, Errol. I can't deny your family was my haven when my parents were too much to handle and the dysphoria was so bad I couldn't breathe under their roof. But dating you was never about that. I'd have dated you if you puked on my shoes, too."

"Gross." I make a face. "We are *not* making getting puked on a sign of affection."

"Birds do it," Rene quips.

"Still not accepting puke in lieu of kisses," I declare, adjusting my glasses.

Rene lets out a bray of laughter. "Once, when Mo was a baby, he got me right in the mouth with baby puke. I leaned in to kiss his chubby little cheeks and he just let loose. It was so gross I can't even adequately describe it."

I chuckle at the story. It's weaker than it should be. I can picture the scene. But along with the pang of regret and loss at not sharing those memories, I can see the humor. I can imagine being there with them. Rene takes in my expression and they sober. They squeeze my hand.

"I'm sorry I took all those little moments away from you, Errol. If I could go back..."

"You can't. We can't. But we can go forward. Make more memories together."

"Like tonight? What is this?" Rene gestures between us. "I don't want a charity date, Errol."

"It's not charity. When was your last evening without Mo?"

"My last hockey game?" Rene says, but it comes out as a question.

"That was your job," I say, exasperated. "I mean the last time you did something fun, just for you?"

Rene shrugs. "Hockey was just for me. It was selfish to stick with it when it took so much of my time and resources."

"Oh, Rene, what am I going to do with you?" I tsk over them.

"Well, considering I can't begin to afford rent and childcare here on my own, I hope you'll keep me," Rene jokes.

"For as long as you want me to," I promise, meaning it with all my heart. We reach the restaurant and get seated at a table near the back. Rene and I fall silent as we peruse the menus and place our orders. Rene orders a margarita with their food, sipping it sparingly as we eat. We keep the conversation light.

Rene asks about my work and my friends, carefully guiding the conversation away from anything that touches on how hard the past few years have been. That taciturn streak is nothing new. They always tried to hide anything that bothered them behind a cheerful facade. It didn't fool me when we were kids, and it doesn't fool me now.

As we're waiting for the bill, I give up prying and ask about introducing Mo to my folks next weekend. I know they'll be thrilled to meet him. My plan is to tell them over the phone first so they have a few days to process the news, then drive down with Mo and Rene first thing on Saturday. Theo will be pissy that I can't play Venture-Quest too late on Friday night, but that's life. As much as I love our gaming group, the game can't be my top priority all the time.

Rene's posture stiffens when I mention all of us going together. "Oh, I'm not sure if that's a good idea."

"Why not?" I ask.

"Because, Errol." They give me an incredulous look, like they can't believe how silly I'm being. "I hurt you. All I've done since we were teenagers is hurt you. How are your parents supposed to react to me being there? I honestly don't know how *you* can be so fucking nice to me considering everything. I can't expect them to forgive me as easily."

"If nothing else, you're Mo's Papa. How could I be anything except nice to you?" I ask, genuinely confused by the reaction.

"In front of him, sure, but you didn't have to take me out to dinner tonight. You could have sent me home and gone out with your son. Catch up on all that lost bonding time with him. You don't have to treat me like a member of your family after—"

"Stop." I set my water down with too much force, frustrated that they don't seem to get it. Rene flinches at the forceful gesture, so I press my hands into the table to still them. I moderate my tone as I say, "You *are* part of my family, Rene. I care about you. Always have, always will."

We're interrupted by the server bringing us our bill. I punch a healthy tip into the machine and tap my card to pay. The server thanks us and leaves.

As we stand to go, I get back to the thread of our conversation. "Did you know I watched every one of your pro games?"

"No. We didn't exactly have a ton of fans. Not compared to the Habs, at least. Where did you even go to find us?" Rene says, they're looking at me with those big wonder-filled eyes that always make me feel ten feet tall.

"I streamed them, or watched them on YouTube if I had to miss the live game," I say simply.

"Jesus, Errol." Rene shakes their head, looking agitated. They clench their fists at their sides. "You can't say shit like that. You're going to break my heart when you realize I'm not worth all this."

"All what?" I ask, stuffing my hands in my pockets to keep myself from reaching for them.

"Everything. You. We shouldn't do this here." Rene gestures around the dining area, so we leave. Once we're on the sidewalk, Rene takes a deep breath, shaking their head at me. "You must realize anyone else wouldn't be giving me the time of day after the way I handled things, right? Heck, I'm sure plenty of people in your position would try to take Mo away from me. And they'd probably win. My folks sure as shit would have fought to get custody of him if they'd known..."

"Never. I'd never try to take you away from him, or

vice versa. And we established a long time ago that your parents have some fucked up ideas." I stop short of telling them how much those ideas have fucked with their head. It's clear enough. I'm also fairly certain their parents have no legal claim to guardianship of Mo, but fears aren't always rational. "You shouldn't have to earn people's love, Rene. That isn't how it's supposed to work."

"Okay," Rene says, disbelief dripping from both syllables, their voice small, brittle with suppressed emotion. We walk a block before I can't leave it alone.

"Name one thing Mo could do to make you stop loving him," I challenge. Rene goes pale at that.

"Nothing." They shake their head.

I nod, point made. Rene won't meet my gaze.

"I never had that, Errol," they say, defeated, shoulders slumping.

"You did," I shoot back, trying to keep the rancor out of my tone. I don't want to agitate them. "Perhaps not from your parents, but you had it."

"I thought that, once," Rene's voice is barely above a whisper, their hurt is palpable in the soft words.

"I never stopped loving you," I insist, gutted at the tacit acknowledgement that my actions, or more to the point, inaction around our breakup, had hurt them. "You're the one who left me."

"You let me," Rene snarls, stopping mid-stride. They tug me to the edge of the sidewalk near a closed shop display, out of the way of anyone who might want to pass. The sidewalks are uncrowded here at this hour. "You let me leave without even asking why."

I could argue that I'd only done what they'd asked for. That they'd left me wounded and grieving my first love. It was the truth. We'd both been so young, immature.

But I'd known Rene. Known that I was the only person they had to turn to. Known those words they flung at me hadn't been sincere. That they must've had a reason to hurt me before they left.

"I'm sorry," I say.

Rene shakes their head and dashes away unshed tears with the back of their hand before I can say more. "Don't apologize. I did it to myself. It's not your fault I'm a fuckup."

"You're not a fuckup, Rene. Tell me about it. What it was like after you left."

"You know what it was like, or you're smart enough to have guessed most of it. I didn't know anyone. I had no idea what I was doing, and I had to settle with seeing the first doctor who could take me. Mo needed me to get prenatal care ASAP. I barely spoke the language, but I could understand enough to realize they misgendered me constantly and aggressively and looked down on me for being young and alone. When I told them I go by Rene, not the name on my health card, they made me spell it out and pronounced it Renée. They had me terrified that if I spoke up about anything, I'd end up delivering Mo alone in my shitty dorm room. I worried they'd take him away from me. The hospital had a social worker check up on me. I lived in fear that my folks would find out and try to take him away. Or cut us off and then I'd lose him or I wouldn't be able to take care of him. I wanted to call you so bad. Every single day." The story tumbles out, Rene's intensity ratcheting up as they talk. They take a ragged breath before continuing.

"I deleted your contact information and blocked you on social media to avoid temptation. And I still punched in your number dozens of times a day for the first couple years. Sometimes I'd call you in the middle of the night, just to get your voicemail so I could hear your voice. I knew you had that stupid thing where your phone blocked notifications after midnight. I figured there was no way you'd be up that late if you had class the next day. After the time you actually picked up, I panicked and stopped. The fucked up part is, I know I deserved to get cut out of your life after what I said, but I was still furious you didn't come after me. You knew where I was. I had this fantasy that I'd be walking to class, or to drop Mo off at the daycare and there you'd be. Every time I glimpsed someone with your build and similar hair, my heart would race for a second, thinking it was you. It was stupid."

I remember the missed calls from a Montreal area code. I convinced myself it must be a particularly awful telemarketer, because the alternative hurt too much to face. The hope they might still care had been too much for my heart to handle back when the wounds of their leaving were still raw. It stings now, to confirm how close we came to reconnecting sooner.

"We can't keep doing this, Rene," I say, running my fingers through my hair to give them something to do other than reaching for Rene.

"Doing what?"

"Hurting each other," I reply. "We're letting all this hurt define our relationship."

"What do you suggest instead? Should we pretend it never happened? That neither of us got hurt?" they demand.

"No." I shove my glasses up my nose, buying time to think. "I don't know. I just know that I still care about you, Rene. More than care." I'd almost forgotten what this sort of attraction felt like, but it was coming back to me along with the love I'd always felt for my best friend. Like riding a bike. "If you still feel the same—"

Rene interrupts me with a kiss that's an answer in itself. At first I'm too stunned to react. I stumble back toward the wall of the building. Rene follows, pinning me against the bricks with another hard press of lips and a hint of teeth. I open to their tongue, letting them lead. They gentle the kiss, fingers digging into my hair as our tongues tangle.

I'm out of practice. The last person I kissed with any actual intent was Rene, and this differs from when we were young.

The soft cheeks that used to carry the roundness of youth are stubbled now, firm under my fingers as I cup their jaw. Their dancing eyes, always alight with mischief, have a wariness they never used to aim toward me.

They still kiss with the same gentle aggression, though. The firm press of their mouth on mine is a persistent demand that I give myself over to them. Let them take us both on a ride that will only end when we've both found our pleasure. I let myself get lost in the movements of their mouth against mine, the way I did before we hurt each other.

A loud whistle and a crude catcall startle us apart. We're on a street. Sure, this is downtown Vancouver, but that doesn't mean there aren't any bigots who might object to us kissing in public. Heck, even if we didn't look like a gay couple, both of us presenting masculine, we're getting a bit too hot and heavy for a sidewalk.

Rene shies away from me, eyes darting around to see if anyone is watching us with hostility. No one seems to have cared enough to linger or give us a hard time.

"Sorry," they mumble, wiping at their mouth.

"Don't be," I say. I take their hand and lead them back toward Pia's place. Anyone else, and this would be the part where I let them down easy. Explain that it's not them, I just don't do sex. Turns out, I can now say with absolute certainty that whatever part of me made Rene turn my crank at seventeen is still firmly stuck on them all these years later. Probably because no matter how bad it hurt to lose them, I never could stop loving them. "Come on. The sooner we get Mo to bed, the sooner we can get back to this conversation."

"Which conversation?" Rene asks, hesitant.

"The one between your tongue and my tonsils," I tease.

Rene crowds closer to me, and I loop an arm around their waist. It means we walk slower, but that's no hardship. "Hm, maybe after that we can revisit the chat between your prostate and my dick," Rene leans in close to whisper the suggestion in my ear.

I tighten my hold around their waist. It's been a heck of a long time. Not that I never get horny or jerk off, but it's rarely a priority. Just a basic need I take care of a couple times a month with my hand in the shower. Tonight, I'm thinking about it. I want Rene in the same way I've wanted them since we first fell in love.

"Bet they've got plenty to say to each other. It's been a damn long time."

"For me, too. It was hell when I went on T. I was a total horndog, I'd have driven you nutters with my libido. I've amassed quite the collection of new toys we can play with, though. Shipped those along with Mo's stuff. It would piss my folks right off to know I spent their money on filthy sex toys. I always got a kick out of that," Rene jokes weakly.

"Way to kill the mood, Rene." I jostle them playfully. "The last person I want to think about when you get back inside me is your dad."

Rene grimaces. "Yeah, forget I said that."

We walk along the sidewalk together for a few blocks, stealing heated glances at each other. It's like I'm the teenager who first fell in love with Rene again as they flash me a nervous smile.

"You sure you're okay with this? I mean, I know you don't—" Rene blurts.

"I do with you," I cut them off. It's the truth. Rene has always been my exception. The only one I've ever wanted sex with. Despite everything about them that has changed since they left, that hasn't. I still love them and I still want them.

"Can we hold off on telling Mo for now?" Rene asks, hand going to their mouth to pick at their ragged nails. "Not forever, just until we're sure what we're doing?"

"You want to hide that we're getting back together from our kid. Our very curious kid, who notices everything. Who we live with?" I ask, raising a skeptical brow. I reach over to pull their hand away from their face, it's an old habit, one I developed because Rene wouldn't stop worrying at their nails until they chewed them down to the sore exposed nail beds if I didn't wordlessly remind them to stop. Rene shoots me a rueful smile as I lace our fingers together.

"Like I said, not for long." Rene shrugs. "Just to be sure we aren't making a mistake."

"If it makes you more comfortable, we can be discreet while we figure out what we're doing," I agree. "Gotta tell you, though, as far as I'm concerned, nothing between us was ever a mistake."

"Sure. Need I remind you of the tequila debacle again?" Rene asks with a derisive snort.

"It was a glorious night. Puke and all. And I'd have taken gallons of puke and a thousand groundings from my folks to keep you safe."

"I'd have been fine," Rene insists, jaw set in a grim line. I hate that I upset them with the reminder.

"Bullshit."

"I got smacked around worse at hockey camp, Errol. I'm tougher than I look," Rene says, ever the stubborn one.

"You never should have had to be."

"I don't want to talk about my folks. In case it wasn't obvious, the only grandparents I want in Mo's life are your parents."

"Done," I agree wholeheartedly with cutting any ties to Rene's parents. "They don't live next to my folks anymore. Sold the house and moved to Kelowna, last I heard, if that's why you don't want to come home with me."

"I heard." Rene offers me a tight-lipped smile as we turn onto Pia's block. "Now, let's fetch our boy and go home. I can't wait to pick up where that kiss left off." They squeeze my hand and their smile turns a little less brittle as our gazes meet. The warmth in their eyes gives me hope that we can rebuild everything that's broken between us.

CHAPTER 12

Rene

I text Emil that we're outside and he meets us at the door with a sleepy-looking Mo and Mo's bag all packed. Mo pouts about saying goodbye to the dog and brags to me about helping Emil fix the baby's bottle earlier. I give him a hug. Errol crouches to greet him, then helps him into the straps of his backpack.

"Mo had a blast and ate his dinner. He picked the chicken out of the lasagna, but he ate the veggies and everything else. So we're considering it a win. He helped Gregor read bedtime stories to Rain. Then we took Otis for a walk, so he got some exercise in, too," Emil reports as Mo bombards Errol with a hug and more chatter about Otis and Rain.

Emil's words make me even more comfortable about letting him watch Mo while I work. It sounds like he'll keep us up to date on what Mo does while he's here, and I appreciate that. Plenty of babysitters I've used in the past would have plunked the kid in front of the TV for the duration of Errol and my evening. Half of the time, they'd have been watching me play hockey. Since my games were one of the few things I've gone out for in the evenings without Mo since his birth.

"Thanks for taking care of him," I say.

"My pleasure, we'll see him on Monday?" Emil checks.

"I'll drop him off like we discussed," Errol agrees. "Tell Pia I can drive them in too, if they want. We can swing by Sin for coffee."

"I bet she'll accept that invitation. Since I'm a moody bas-," Emil cuts his eyes to the kid and changes what he was going to say, "-dude about having coffee smells in the house right now. I'm supposed to be cutting back on caffeine."

"No caffeine and an eight-month-old? You're braver than me," I joke.

"It'll be worth it," Emil gives me a tight smile. "Anyway, I'm sure Mo will be a great helper, won't you, kiddo?"

"I'm going to be a great big brother," Mo agrees solemnly.

"How about you be a good big honorary cousin to Rain?" Errol suggests.

Mo wrinkles his nose. "I don't have cousins."

"Well, technically, no. Papa and Daddy don't have any siblings, so you don't have cousins by blood. But Pia and Emil and Gregor are like siblings to Daddy, so Rain is like your cousin," Errol explains.

Mo considers that and then nods, "Okay. Bye, Uncle Emil." He waves.

Emil waves back. He shoots Errol a smile. "See you Monday, Mo."

Mo falls asleep in the car and Errol carries him into his

room without waking him up. It's weird to watch someone else holding my kid like he's the most precious person on the planet. Weird, but good. It scares me that I'm getting used to it. Used to watching Errol tuck Mo in and kiss his forehead.

It terrifies me that getting back together with Errol could mark the beginning of the end of this fragile new thing between the three of us. What if we don't work anymore? Errol could decide he doesn't want me around. Kick me out. Take Mo. I can't handle that possibility.

Errol's hands on my shoulders make me flinch out of my racing thoughts. He brushes his lips over mine, gentle and achingly familiar, even after all the years apart.

"Come to my room?" he asks.

I give a stiff nod and cling to his hand as he leads the way. I haven't ventured inside his bedroom yet. It feels like intruding. I'm already an interloper in his home, I wanted to at least preserve some privacy for him. Errol shoots me a questioning look when I balk at his door.

"What's wrong?" Errol asks.

I bite my lip and shake my head, knowing I'm acting stupid. "What if this ruins things?"

"It won't." Errol says, with enough conviction to decide me. "It's just sex. If you don't want it, we don't have to. You know I'm happy to keep it to kissing and cuddles. Or we can say goodnight and you can go to your room if you prefer."

It's not what I prefer. I want Errol so badly that it's a dull ache in my chest and my nether bits. I swallow down my doubts and grasp my courage. "Let's try."

Errol pulls me close and kisses my neck. I tilt my head away to give him access. "Tell me what you like," he murmurs, breath tickling my skin as he peppers my throat in kisses between the words.

"You. I like you." I grip his shoulders, needing to connect with him.

"Need you to be a bit more specific, imzadi," Errol says dryly. That corny old endearment brings tears to my eyes. I never thought I'd hear it from his lips again. His beloved.

Errol skims his mouth along my jaw to the ticklish spot behind my ear that always makes me squirm, defusing the tumble of emotions inside me. From the familiar grin he gives me when I writhe away, he remembered that little tidbit. I shove him.

"See? You remember," I complain.

"Yep, turns out riding you is like riding a bike," Errol agrees with a broad wink. "How do you want to do this?"

"Naked," I suggest. Definitely naked. I want to see him again. Errol steps away and strips his shirt over his head, flinging it toward his laundry hamper. Then he drops his pants and boxers, steps out of them and whips them toward the hamper too.

I take in his lanky form. He's got more muscle than the last time I saw him. And more coarse dark hair covers his chest and thighs. His dick is only half hard, nestled in more dark wiry hair. I kind of want to bury my face in his crotch and enjoy the bristle of his pubes on my skin, experience my stubble rasping against it. Breathe in the musky scent of him where it will be most potent.

Errol clears his throat. "My eyes are up here, sailor."

"Yeah, I got that, but I'm looking at your dick, stud," I shoot back. Errol chuckles.

"You can do more than look."

"I want to taste," I say.

"Go for it," Errol gestures toward his dick.

I close the distance between us and kiss him instead of going right for his dick. He moans into my mouth and presses against me. I pull away and slide down his body to kneel at his feet. Errol rests a gentle hand on top of my head and murmurs sweet nothings as I take his dick in my hand and lick a stripe over the smooth head. He's still a bit flaccid, but I don't mind. I love the feel of him getting firm against my tongue, so I don't waste any time sucking him into my mouth.

I take my time playing with his glans, licking and sucking until the tang of his pre-cum hits my taste buds. Then I take him deeper, bobbing along his shaft and loving the way he swells and grows in my mouth as he gets into it.

I moan around him and Errol's hand in my hair urges me closer. He's still gentle, always gentle with me.

"Close, Rene, so close, imzadi," Errol warns. He pats my cheek.

I pull back, keeping just the tip in my mouth. I gaze up, meeting his eyes. It's intense, looking up into his adoring gaze while I've got him in my mouth. I tongue at his slit. Errol groans, he cups the back of my head and for an instant I can imagine him forcing me down. Claiming my mouth and throat and using me. That's never been us, though.

Errol urges me away. He closes his eyes as I replace my mouth with my fist and jerk him a little to keep him hard.

"Want to fuck me?" I offer.

"Not tonight. I want you inside me tonight, Rene."

"I'm, uh, a bit different there, too," I say. It's not that I think that will matter to Errol, but it's still a vulnerable truth to share.

"Yeah?" Errol asks. He offers me an encouraging smile.

"Yeah. After Mo I, uh, had way more going on up here,"

I make a vague sweeping gesture toward my chest. "It was—not great for my mental health. Got to where I could barely stand to have Mo hug me before I got surgery. It was a pain in the ass to schedule around hockey season. Top surgery helped for a while. Enough to delay starting hormones while I played. The league was good about my pronouns and identity stuff, but they were—uh, difficult?—about my hormone levels around playing. Had to retire for the rest of my transition related stuff, but I'm happy with the results."

"Is that why you hung up your skates?" Errol asks. He's softening in my hand as we talk, and I'm irritated that we can't just jump into sex. That it's complicated for us both.

"Yeah. That and the lack of pay. Can't support a kid on a job that doesn't pay. With the time requirements, it was hard to hold another job around my league responsibilities. It's a miracle I made it work for one season. I don't want to chat about it. Just giving you a heads-up that I've changed down below." I jerk him more firmly, hoping to get him hard again.

Errol nudges my hand away, then tugs me to my feet. He takes my face between his hands and kisses me on the mouth, his tongue teasing my lips open until I let him control the kiss. He pulls away when I let myself lean into his naked body.

"That doesn't matter to me. Not beyond you being happy with it. You know I'm into *you*, not your parts," Errol says, searching my eyes to see if I believe him.

"Yeah. Okay," I glance away.

"Take off your clothes and let me see you, Rene," Errol says. The words are a demand, but his soft tone makes it a question.

I strip for him. Nothing sexy about it, just clothes coming off in a heap on the floor. Errol's eyes on me say he likes what he sees. I lift my arms and let him get a good look at me. "So, yeah, this is me."

Errol's lips quirk up, "I love you."

That's not a declaration I dared allow myself to hope I'd ever hear from him again. Hot tears prick the backs of my eyes at the overwhelming emotion his words bring up. "Why?"

Errol pulls me tight against his body. My dick bumps against his. It's not as though it's huge, even after the simple release surgery that shaped it, but it's mine. The enticing sensation of Errol hardening between us as my erect dick rubs against his sends a thrill of pleasure through me.

"You're still my Rene. The kid I rode bikes with every day. The kid who helped me build the tree fort. My first everything."

"The dumbass who constantly dragged you into trouble." I add with a choked laugh.

"My best friend. I've missed you. Every day since you left. I don't want to waste any more time missing you. Come to bed and show me how you want me to touch you these days."

"Tonight, I just want to hold you against my body while we kiss."

"Frot too, or no?" Errol asks.

"Yeah." I nod my agreement, humping into him.

"Okay. Whatever you want." Errol draws me to the bed and we separate long enough to slide between the sheets, then we find each other again, lips locking, bodies writhing together. Errol gets our dicks lined up and strokes us with his pre-cum as slick. It's clear I still turn him on, even after everything that's come between us.

It's incredible to have his hard-on rubbing along the underside of mine. I've fantasized about this. I can't hold back my gasps of pleasure. His lips stifle my moans, even as I fuck my tongue into his mouth and my dick against his. It's a moment of perfect bliss as our bodies connect. Mine finally feels right pressed against his. It's just us here, Errol and I bringing each other pleasure with no other concerns. No fear of discovery or punishment. No worry that he will see me as something I'm not based on the parts I'm rubbing against him. Just our bodies moving as one, reduced to the pleasure singing along our nerves and our hearts beating in time.

I don't know which of us comes first, just that we're a wet sticky mess when it's over. I still don't want to pull away or give up having his lips on mine. Errol must agree, because the cum puddling between us gets smeared everywhere by the time we break our lip lock, and our hands cease wandering.

"We should clean up before we fall asleep," Errol says.

"I should go back to my bed," I say, reluctant. The only thing I've ever meant less was our breakup.

"Stay," Errol urges me.

"Mo will know." I bite my lip, wanting to give in to his request.

"Stay anyway. I don't want to sneak around, Rene. I've spent too many years not being able to touch you or kiss you when I want to. Don't ask me to hide this from our son."

"You sure? What if—" I fret. Errol cuts me off with a demanding kiss.

"No more what ifs. You're the love of my life. Nothing can change that. We've still got the chemistry, I don't need more time to think or decide. I'm all in with you."

"Same," I agree.

"So, stay?" he presses.

"Yeah. Okay. We should still clean up, though. Don't want Mo to wake up and try to snuggle with us only to end up in the wet patch," I say.

"Yeah, gross. Okay, you can use the ensuite while I change the sheets," Errol says. He rolls out of bed and goes to get a fresh set of sheets from his closet.

I only drag myself out of his plush bed with great reluctance. It's as soft as a cloud compared to the lumpy futon in my tiny makeshift room. Not that I'm complaining, Errol's giving me a place to stay out of the goodness of his heart. Few exes would be anywhere near as accommodating as him.

I agreed to sleep with him in his big comfortable bed, but I keep second-guessing that choice as I help myself to the roomy walk-in shower in his en suite. This washroom is nicer than the narrow shower stall in the other bathroom. There's a deep soaker tub and two sinks. It's like something my parents would have had. All grown up and professional.

There's room in the shower for two, so I linger soaping my body. Errol doesn't follow me inside, so I end up rinsing off and wrapping myself in one of his plush towels in neutral tones that match the beige tiles. Like something lifted straight from a home design magazine. Or one of the decorating shows we used to watch, and throw harsh judgments at, as teens. When I step out of the steamy washroom and into the bedroom, Errol is sitting on his bed. He has a pair of my pajamas laid out for me, a tacit reminder of his invitation to stay.

"Didn't think you'd mind me going into your room for

clothes, hope that's ok?" Errol gestures at the PJs.

"More than. Thanks, stud." I lean in to peck his cheek and he turns into the kiss, meeting my lips with his. There's no sexual intent there, just affection and warmth. "You could have joined me."

"Were you lonely, Rene?" Errol teases.

"Very. Next time keep me company, stud," I tease back.

"I will, now that I know it would be welcome. Let me rinse off and I'll be right back. Make yourself comfortable."

I intend to wait up for him, but I'm snoring the minute my head hits the pillows. Errol's bed is the most comfortable I've slept on in ages, not even counting the futon. I could get used to this.

CHAPTER 13

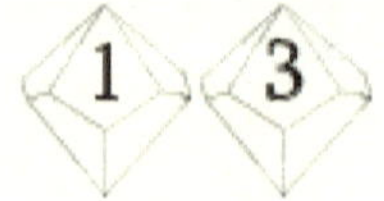

Errol

It's not the first time I've woken up with Rene in my bed. As teens, that always proved a risky proposition. It usually meant we'd fallen asleep somewhere we shouldn't have, like our tree fort, or my parents' basement. A few times it was in my room after a late night. Rene's teammate, Caro, usually covered for us by telling Rene's folks the two of them were having a sleepover.

Once, I'd stayed the night in Rene's room when their parents were out of town for an anniversary trip. Every single time we woke up together in the past, Rene bailed fast to get to where they were supposed to be and avoid trouble with their parents.

This lovely Friday, Rene is sleeping sprawled across my bed when Mo knocks on the door fifteen minutes before my alarm is set to ring.

"Daddy, Papa's missing," he calls through my door on the verge of panic. Then he barges in before I can reply. He freezes in the doorway at the sight of us together in the bed.

“Papa?” Mo takes a tentative step toward us. Beside me, Rene sits up.

“Hey, Momo, didn’t mean to scare you, bud,” Rene rubs sleep from their eyes and lifts the blankets in invitation. “Come snuggle for a minute, Daddy’s bed is the comfiest.”

Mo scampers around to Rene’s side of the mattress and dives atop the blankets to snuggle in. Rene rolls Monet in between us and wraps an arm around the kid, kissing his cheeks until he cries uncle.

“Stop,” Mo giggles and shoves Rene’s head away. Rene stops. “You can’t distract me with kisses! Why are you in Daddy’s bed?”

“I would never try to distract anyone with kisses, Momo, what are you implying?” Rene says with mock outrage. Mo rolls his eyes.

“You do, too. Daddy, why is Papa sleeping in your room? Are you two dating? Uncle Emil said you weren’t on a date last night, just having dinner together, but Pia —if Emil is my honorary uncle, does that make Pia my auntie now?”

“Yeah,” I agree. “Emil’s niblings call them Auntie Pia. You can ask her on Monday, to be sure it’s okay, though.”

“Okay. Auntie Pia said to ask you if it was a date. So, are you two dating? Does this mean I get a baby sibling after all?” Mo asks, cutting right to the part that interests him.

“We are dating.” I admit.

“And we’ve already got a perfect kid, what do we need with another one?” Rene jokes, tousling Mo’s hair. He rolls his eyes and tries to fix his cowlick.

“Because then you could have two perfect kids,” Mo retorts, sticking out his tongue at Rene.

"Let's have breakfast, since we're all up," Rene suggests, avoiding a direct answer as they climb out of bed. "What do you say, Momo? Want to help me mix the pancake batter while Daddy gets ready for work?"

"Okay," Mo agrees. He follows Rene to the kitchen. I take Rene's suggestion and grab a quick shower before dressing and joining them in the kitchen.

This time, when I walk in on the domestic scene, I don't resist the urge to wrap my arms around Rene's waist and kiss their neck. They lean back into me with a pleased sound, but don't turn away from trying to draw with the pancake batter.

"That's not a very good car, Papa," Mo observes.

"He's right," I agree the pancake is more of an oblong blob than anything identifiable.

"You try then, mister artist," Rene grumbles, turning to shove the bottle full of batter into my hands. Then they give me a peck on the lips and abandon me to our art critic son. Rene fixes me a cup of coffee while I flip the first fail car. The coffee, prepared just the way I prefer, helps me forgive Rene for thrusting me into the hot seat.

I plate the car and slide it to Rene, then I do my best to make our kid a couple of car-shaped pancakes. They won't win any awards, but it makes him smile, so that's enough reward for my efforts.

Rene jokes that they want a motorcycle, but I make them hockey pucks. Their eyes dance with amusement even as they complain that Mo's pancakes look better.

"You could at least do a skate, or hockey sticks or something," Rene grumbles.

"You should have a *Battle Fox*," Mo suggests when it's my turn. I pour the batter into the shape of a generic video game controller to appease him.

"Next time you should do the creepy eyeball logo from your job," Rene suggests

"Noted," I say. We need to buy food dye to color the batter for the details if this is going to be a thing, our first family tradition. At least it distracts Mo from begging us to have another kid or get a dog. I'm not opposed to the idea of giving the kid a sibling, or a pet.

If I'm honest, part of me wants the chance to have all those missed milestones. I realize having another kid won't erase those missing years with Mo. It's obvious that Rene struggled with carrying him. I don't know if they would be open to another pregnancy. For all I know, they might have taken permanent steps to prevent it.

Besides, Rene and I are still figuring out how to be together as a couple again. It's way too soon to even be considering more kids. But maybe someday?

"The studio has a happy hour tonight. I should be home close to the usual time, but I might grab a drink with the gang and give Laura a ride home. So I might be later than usual, if that's alright?" I say.

"Of course. You planning on eating with us?" Rene asks.

"Yes. If you want, we can order in so you don't have to cook," I suggest.

"I don't mind," Rene hedges.

"Pizza!" Mo crows cxcitedly.

Rene bites their lip and I can see them calculating the cost of delivery. I slide my credit card out of my wallet and pass it to Rene. I've got enough cash on me for lunch.

"Order whatever you two like," I say, then I kiss them firmly on the lips to forestall any argument. Rene sighs.

"I'll buy next time," they say, and I don't fight them on it, knowing it's a matter of pride. I leave for work a little late and more content than I recall being in ages. If tonight is anything like the last couple of weeks, I've got an evening full of laughter, fun, and games with Rene and Mo to look forward to. It's not quite like old times, it's better.

CHAPTER 14

1 4

Errol

I arrive home at the same time as our pizza. I didn't spend long mingling at my work sponsored happy hour. Just snagged free snacks and soda and chatted with a few co-workers. Laura didn't end up needing a ride since she has plans with Alice.

After dinner and a few rounds of *Battle Fox,* I read Mo his favorite dinosaur book. I spend half the book mentally cursing the scientists who decided every name in the pages needed to be unpronounceable by mortal tongues. Rene asks if I want help with the bedtime routine, but it's nice to have one-on-one time with Mo and they deserve alone time to unwind. I tuck Mo into his bed and kiss his forehead.

Once Mo's all set for the night, I find Rene watching a hockey movie on their ancient laptop in the living room. I lean over them, brushing my lips over their brow. They pause the movie.

"Come to our bed?" I suggest. That little slip of the tongue, calling it ours instead of mine, earns me a heated smile and a scorching kiss.

We move to the bedroom, but we make out instead of watching the movie. Rene climbs on top of me, straddling my hips and rubbing our dicks together until they come in their pants. I hold them on top of me for a while until their breathing evens out into sleep. Then I roll them to the side and get myself ready for bed.

Not that I don't enjoy the sex, just coming isn't the primary aim for me. When we were younger, we talked about it a lot. How I'd always felt broken when other guys talked about popping wood over celebrities, or wanting to get in a pretty girl's pants.

Rene was the first person I ever saw that way; as someone I desired sexually. I didn't learn the words that fit me and made me feel less alone until university. Demisexual and panromantic. But even before I had the language to explain myself, Rene listened, tried to understand as best they could. The only time Rene ever made me feel inadequate over my sexuality or my lack of libido was the day we broke up. It's why that day was so awful for me.

From the time we started dating, I've been into fooling around with Rene. I enjoy kissing and physical intimacy with them. Sex was part of our relationship because orgasms feel good. On the other hand, so does a hot bath, and baths are considerably less messy.

When we first got together, Rene used to worry about asking for sex, thinking I'd agree just to make them happy. We had a lot of conversations about sex. Rene always had a higher libido than me. They liked to jerk off daily. Getting off every day sounded like a chore to me. Stolen kisses with Rene, and exchanging tender touches while letting them rub off against my body, or next to me, was never a chore. That hasn't changed.

As far as sex goes, I'm in no hurry to move beyond frottage and making out in bed. That's as far as things progress over the weekend. It's nice to reconnect sexually, as well as emotionally, though. I enjoy having Rene in my arms all night.

Waking up to our kid climbing in the bed to snuggle between us in the morning isn't half bad either. Monday morning, Mo and I get up early to make Rene pancakes. This time, I go all out drawing the logo for their new junior team with different colors of batter.

Rene is a ball of nerves, but they chuckle at the food art and kiss us both on the cheeks. Mo rubs off the kiss, making a silly face. I pull Rene into my arms and claim a proper kiss, with our tongues tangling, until Mo makes a gagging sound. He tells us to get a room. The kid sounds more giggly than grossed out, though.

After breakfast, we all pile into my car. I drop Rene off for their first day at the sports complex where the team practices, before taking Mo to Emil's place. I snap a 'first day' selfie for my folks, knowing they'll want pictures of their grandson as soon as I tell them they have one. Today is the day I change their lives the way Rene did mine. And, wow, how can only two full weeks have passed since I met Mo?

Pia joins me for the drive to work after I drop off Mo. She's mumbling about coffee as she buckles into the passenger seat. I park by the curb at Sin and Chocolate so we can get our caffeine fix from Pascal. Pia perks up after a few sips.

"How was your weekend?" she asks.

"Great." I grin over at them. "You know how I told you

Friday at lunch that I wasn't sure if Rene moving into my room was a one time fluke or if they wanted more?"

"Yeah?" She arches a brow, encouraging me to elaborate.

"Well, they've been staying in my room. So, I think we're going to try this again for real."

"I'm glad for you, Errol." Pia slugs me in the bicep. I rub the spot she hit with a pout. They chuckle at me.

"Ouch," I complain. We get back in the car to drive the distance from Sin and Chocolate to the studio.

"Oh, hush, you big baby. You seem happy with them. I wasn't sure what to think when you said your ex had returned out of the blue with a kid they claimed was yours. I mean, other than that it was some serious soap opera bullshit going on. But then I met Rene, and I've never seen you smile about anyone the way you smile about them, so I'm happy for you, Errol."

"Thanks, Pea. I'm happy for me, too. How's everything with your family?" I ask, deflecting. I don't want to jinx this thing with Rene and I. It's too new and precious to share more than the broad strokes. Not even with the friends who have become my chosen family.

"We're good. I'm a better parent now that I've reclaimed my work life. The antidepressants don't hurt, either." Pia winks at me. "Postnatal hormones are a bitch. It also helps that Rain is interacting more. They'll giggle if we play peek-a-boo or clap and wave when they see me. Other than that, Gregor and I are low-key bracing for how Emil will react if the IVF doesn't work out this round."

"Yeah. When is the first round?" I ask, checking my blind spot before changing lanes.

"He's just finishing up with the oral contraceptives this week. He hates this part, even though it's standard to start the cycle with a clean slate, so to speak." Pia grimaces, and I'm familiar enough with the strain all these fertility treatments put on their family to empathize with that unspoken frustration. She sips her coffee. "So we're moving on to the nightly injections and every-other-day blood draws and ultrasounds at the clinic later this week to monitor follicles. On that note, Rain and Mo will join us for lunch so Emil can get to the clinic Tuesday and Thursday next week."

"Oh, no, I think Mo has his hockey camp during the day next week, so that's one less thing for Emil to worry about on top of the testing," I interject.

"That works out, then. Good timing." Pia nods their head agreeably. "In an ideal world, the retrieval should be the following week? They said 15 days at the outside. Depending on how things look, they'll implant an egg around day five after fertilization or freeze them for later. We're hoping to have enough to freeze extras, for if this round doesn't work. Should know our results by the end of September? Again, if all goes well."

"Good luck. If you need help to distract Emil, or cheer him up, or for us to take Rain for a night or a weekend, let me know, okay?" I offer.

"You sure?" Pia asks. As well she might, I've babysat for them with Laura, but never for more than a couple hours.

"Yeah," I nod, warming to the idea. "I think Mo would kill to get a chance at playing big brother for an entire night," I joke.

"We might take you up on that. Depends how things go. Thanks, dude." Pia smacks my shoulder.

I park in the underground lot at the studio in my reserved space.

"You coming in?" Pia asks when I dawdle behind the

wheel.

"You can go on without me, I need to tell my folks about Monet." I sip from my hot coffee to hide my nerves about that conversation. Pia pats my thigh sympathetically.

"Want me to stay for moral support?" she asks, seeing right through my calm facade.

"Nah, it's fine. They'll be over the moon, once they get their heads around him existing. Surprised, but thrilled." I wave away their offer of support.

Pia nods, squeezing my shoulder. "I'm a call away if you need someone afterward, okay?"

"I'll let you know how it goes," I promise. "Thanks, Pea."

I watch as Pia takes their coffee into the building. They glance back and blow me a kiss before disappearing into the stairwell. With nothing left to distract me, I pick up my phone and dial. Mom answers on the third ring.

"Is everything alright, Errol?" Mom asks. Her familiar voice makes me smile.

"Yeah. Everything is perfect." I scrub my free hand through my hair. "I just have some news. You can't freak out, okay?"

"Did something happen with your work?" Mom asks.

"No. Work is good. Listen, you remember Rene, right?" I hold my breath for her response.

Mom's breath catches and I can picture her concerned expression as she warily asks, "Are they back in town?"

"Yeah. They got a job working with the Oilers, the juniors team based in Burnaby. They're staying with me."

"Oh, Errol, baby, no," Mom says. It's not a shock. Mom was there for the argument that broke my heart and, to her mind, kept me from dating for the past seven years.

"It's not what you think," I protest.

"Are you getting back together with them?" Mom demands, and I can tell she wants to add, 'tell me you aren't,' but she refrains from passing judgment. Well, more judgment than that.

I sigh, pinching the bridge of my nose. This isn't how I wanted this conversation to progress. "I love them. I've always loved them, and they had their reasons for leaving the way they did."

"Reasons that excuse the things they called you? Tell me," Mom demands.

"You can't get angry at them over this, Mom, promise?" I plead.

"Over *what*, Errol?" Mom's words sound clipped. I wish I could do this in person, but I need my folks to have time to cool off before they see Rene again. Mo deserves better than to have his first memories of them tainted by my folks' fears about Rene hurting me again.

"You remember what their parents were like?" I ask, hoping to play on mom's sympathy.

"Yes."

"Then you recall how strict they were. How scared Rene was to step out of line, right?"

"What happened, Errol?" Mom demands.

"They left like they did because we..." I swallow hard, god this is hard to say. It's going to break her heart the same way it broke mine. And she'll get past it when she meets Mo, like I did.

"You what, my boy?" Mom's voice softens, reminding me of the way she used to make everything better when I was a little kid. That warmth lets me blurt out the truth.

"We made a kid. Monet. He's six and a half. Bilingual, because they raised him in Quebec until this month. And he's this perfect, tiny person. He likes pancakes, and cars, and Ollie Owl. He calls me Daddy and you can't be mad at his papa because I love them both more than I thought I could love anyone. So, yeah, I'm sorry it happened this way, but congratulations, you're a grandma."

Dead silence greets my manic description. It goes on long enough that I hold the phone away from my ear to be sure we haven't gotten disconnected.

"A grandson?" Mom repeats, emotion raw in her voice. It's hard to say if it's grief or wonder, but it's intense and I can relate to not knowing how to process the news. After another beat of silence, she draws in a shaky breath and repeats, "You have a son? And they named him Monet?"

"We call him Mo," I say, getting defensive on Rene's behalf.

"Mo," Mom tests out his nickname. "Okay. I can live with that. Mo," she repeats, tone warming. "You're sending me pictures as soon as we hang up, and I expect a visit as soon as possible. We've got years of spoiling to make up for, text me his favorite cookies."

"And you'll be nice to Rene?" I check.

Mom sighs. "Give me time? They hurt you, baby. And then they hid your baby from you, that's a lot to forgive."

"I'm the one they hurt the most, and I've forgiven them for it. But I get it, I was mad when they told me, too. I understand if you need time to process. Just try to understand that Rene did the best they could, under the circumstances. And no matter how mad or hurt you are, I won't tolerate anyone badmouthing Rene in front of Mo. Are we clear?"

"Yes," Mom agrees. Then her tone softens again. "I'm so proud of you, Errol. You're a good man, and I have no doubt you are an amazing dad. I can't wait to meet Mo."

"We'll bring him home to visit this weekend, if that works for you and Dad?"

"That works. Should I set up the extra cot in the guestroom or will Rene be sharing with you?" Mom asks stiffly. She's trying to accept this. That's all I can ask.

"With me," I state, brooking no argument.

"Alright. Do you want to tell your father, or shall I?" Mom asks. I consider the time; I need to get to work, but it's not every day you tell your folks you have a kid.

"Is he around?" I ask.

"He's just headed out the door, want me to give him the phone?"

"Yes, please. Love you, Mom."

"To the moon," Mom shoots back, then she gives the phone to my father.

"Errol, my boy, what's the occasion?" Dad asks.

"Can't a son just call to say he loves his parents?" I joke.

"Sure, but it's rare for you to call before work on a weekday." He has a point.

"I don't know how much of what I said to Mom you overheard, but Rene contacted me two weeks ago."

"And? Are you two getting back together?" Dad asks, skeptical. "You know what I say about exes, son. You broke up for a reason."

"Yeah, well, the reason in this case is your grandson. Rene left to hide the pregnancy from their folks. And you can guess how they'd have reacted."

Dad sighs, I can picture him running his hands through his thinning hair at that. I think between my parents, Dad will have the easier time forgiving Rene. He saw the bruises Rene always blamed on hockey practice. Maybe some of them were truly from the ice, but I drove them home from practice and more than once they collected new bruises between trips to the rink. "He'd be six then?"

"Almost seven," I agree.

"That must have been hard to hear. Did you know when they left?" Dad asks.

"If I'd known about him, I'd have been there for Rene and Mo," I say, sharper than I should.

"I don't doubt that," Dad says in a soothing tone. "Well, I'm looking forward to meeting him. You tell Rene I say hi and that they're welcome to visit anytime, this is still their home and no one will make them feel unwanted here, alright?"

"Thanks, Dad. That will mean the world to them."

"Do Rene's parents know?"

"No. We'd prefer it to stay that way for as long as possible. So, if you could convince Mom not to post all over social media about Mo..."

"I'm on it," Dad says. "Send your mother pictures; she's beside herself already."

"Happy?" I check.

"Thrilled. This is good news, Errol. I'll make sure she remembers that."

"Thanks, Dad."

"Proud of you, son."

I hang up and share my phone's photo album with Mom so she can ogle all the pics of Mo I've taken in the past few weeks. It's a lot of pictures, but I'm pretty sure new parents get a pass on hoarding photos of their kids.

CHAPTER 15

1 5

Rene

My first week of work flies past. It's amazing to be back on the ice at the practice rink. For now, I'm working with kids at a summer camp. I've missed the smell of the ice, sweat and cold and that certain something I can't describe that feels like coming home.

Before I met Errol, the only place I could be myself was with blades strapped to my feet. Even in my peewee league, the bulky jersey and pads covering my body made me feel safe. Like they could erase the blurred lines between boys and girls and make us all simply hockey players.

That sense of the ice being my home never left. Not even when I had to delay the medical side of my transition to meet league rules. Hockey was always there for me, giving me what I needed.

The camp our team is running is meant to drum up

interest in little kids to develop young talent. Next week we're running a camp for Mo's age group and I've already filled out the paperwork to get him enrolled, if he's interested. I hope Errol won't object. My boss already told me he'd waive the registration fees and overlook the enrollment deadline for my kid, since we just moved.

The camp will rent him most of the equipment he'll need. So, with my first paycheck hitting my account soon, I can swing the costs without asking Errol for more handouts. Not that asking him to cover costs for our kid is a handout, but I'm not used to sharing responsibility for Monet. I've never had to check with someone else about parenting decisions before. It's strange, but good.

And speaking of shared responsibilities, I've got to get out of here on time tonight because it's Friday and Errol has his game night. That leaves me in charge of picking up Mo from Emil's place. My boss catches me on the way out the door and I brace for whatever he might have to say to me.

"Excellent work this week, Dumond, you're great with the kids, glad we took a chance on you," he says, nodding at me.

"Thanks." I flash a tentative smile. "Mo has me used to working with the younger kidlets. I can't wait to work with our actual team after the summer recess," I say honestly.

"Glad to have you on board." He claps me on the shoulder. "Enjoy your weekend."

I try to hide my nervous grimace at what this weekend has in store. Coach gives me a questioning look and I explain, "We're bringing Mo to visit with his other dad's folks this weekend."

"Ah." He chuckles. "I can relate to that face now. A

weekend with the in-laws, huh?"

"Something like that," I agree with a rueful shake of my head. It's close enough to describing who they are to me. I'm too relieved that he doesn't care that I'm with a man to drag out the sordid details of my past after the first week working with the man. Then again, he knew all about my transition history when he hired me. Since my hockey career was in the women's league, disclosure seemed unavoidable. We say our goodbyes and I get another manly clap on the back before I duck out to pick up Mo and get him packed for our weekend trip.

CHAPTER 16

Errol

We plan to leave for my parent's place before dawn on Saturday morning. Theo is grumpy that I cut our game session short at ten, but he's a drama queen. He was already complaining over a prank Jude and Pia pulled earlier in the session. Jude distracts him from his irritation with promises of going out dancing and the rest of the gang are all on board, so it's not like I'm ruining his night.

Besides, our party ended the session camped outside of the tower where the mercenaries are keeping the captive dragon prince we're trying to rescue. It's a great stopping point that gives us plenty of time to prepare for the BBEG encounter in the next few sessions.

The relatively early hour gives me time to get home and get packed for our trip. And save Rene's nails from getting chewed to the quick with nerves over seeing my folks again. They glance up at me guiltily when I walk into the room, hiding their hands behind their back. They're crouched over a suitcase that is overflowing with unfolded clothing.

"You're going to make yourself bleed again if you keep that up, Rene," I chastise them with a soft smile.

Rene grimaces. "I tried to quit, doesn't stick."

"It's fine. Can I help get your mind off the nerves?"

"They're going to hate me," Rene wails.

"They're going to love Mo so much they won't even notice us," I counter, taking their hands and drawing them into a tight hug.

"What if they can't forgive me?"

"They will learn to at least pretend real damn good if they want to be part of Mo's life," I state.

"You mean that?" Rene asks.

"Yes. Their feelings are their business, but if they treat you with anything less than respect, we will pack up and leave," I promise.

"Why do you have to be so perfect for me?" Rene grumbles. I can tell they're still anxious. So I kiss them again, long and gentle, until Rene takes charge, thrusting their tongue deep into my mouth. They cling to my body and press their erection into my hip. Well, if that isn't an obvious clue about how to keep them distracted, I don't know what is. I break off the kiss and push Rene toward the bed.

They lay back with a low chuckle. "Can I help you, stud?"

"Yeah, as a matter of fact, you can, get your pants off and let me suck your pretty new cock," I say, brushing hair out of their eyes. Rene pulls me down on top of them for another rough kiss.

"You sure?"

"Yes, imzadi, make it so," I say.

They get their pants off and I fasten my lips around their erect dick. It's more than a mouthful, and I enjoy the feel and taste of Rene on my tongue. I love the way they writhe under me. Gripping my hair to hold me close, bucking off the bed as I drive them wild with my tongue. It's fun to wring their pleasure out of them until their dick gets impossibly hard and they groan my name with their fists balled tight in my hair. I press my face as close to their body as I can get, nose buried in their pubes. They hold me in place until they're going limp in my mouth, orgasm achieved and their eyes heavy lidded as they stroke my hair.

"You can fuck me, if you want," Rene offers in a sleepy voice that breaks on a yawn.

I chuckle at the perfunctory offer, but I'm not really in the mood for more. "Another time, I think. Sleep, we've got an early morning."

"If you're sure," Rene wriggles around to get under the covers. They don't push, they never do when it comes to sex, a fact I appreciate.

"I'm sure. Get to sleep, I'll finish packing."

"My hero," Rene teases. They watch me as I fix the explosion of clothing trailing out of their suitcase. I make sure they have everything they might need for a weekend with my folks, then add my clothing and toiletries, since there is still plenty of space left over. I zip it up to add it to the pile of Mo's things stacked in our entryway.

The boxes full of toys and extra clothing that Rene shipped before moving arrived a few days ago. So between that and the gifts my friends bought, Mo has more stuff now. If I know my mom at all, he'll return from this visit loaded down with even more gifts and goodies.

That's okay. Mom's right, we've got years of spoiling the kid to make up for.

When I join Rene under the covers, they hug me tight and kiss me softly until I fall asleep, my face tingling pleasantly with beard burn from all the kissing. It's just what I needed to feel connected with them before we face whatever the weekend might bring.

I meant what I said about leaving if my folks make Rene uncomfortable. Rene and Mo are my priority, but it will suck if this weekend doesn't go well. I want my folks to have a relationship with my kid. Hopefully our visit is pleasant.

CHAPTER 17

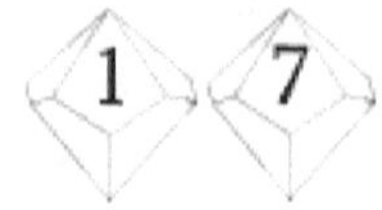

Rene

Errol drives the car. We stop for breakfast at Tim Horton's on the way out of the city. Mo gets car-sick on long rides, a fact I found out the hard way years ago. It's a pain in the ass to clean vomit out of a car seat, and the smell always lingers no matter how much disinfectant I use. So I give him some Dramamine with his bagel and box of Timbits. The meds zonk the kid out like a light for most of the long drive.

Errol and I chat a bit at first, but as we get closer to our destination, I'm too full of nerves to follow the thread of conversation. He eventually gives up and puts on an audiobook. Something humorous and nonfiction, but I can't focus on that either. My mind keeps wandering to where we're going and everything that little town represents. Errol rests a hand on my thigh and I squeeze it. He doesn't offer platitudes or false reassurances before he returns both hands to the wheel. I appreciate that. He's just there for me.

I take solace in that knowledge, that no matter what I do, Errol's always in my corner. It only increases my regret over not telling him about Mo sooner. Except he's made a wonderful life for himself in Vancouver. My pregnancy would have screwed that up, if I'd told him about it. I made the right choice from a practical career standpoint. It just hurt us both a hell of a lot more than I thought it would.

The closer we get to our old hometown, the more my mind wanders down memory lane. I hate going there. I'd be content never to step foot back in the place where I hurt Errol, but his family is there and Mo deserves a relationship with Errol's folks.

They were always good to me, even the first day Errol brought me home, covered in dirt and twigs from playing in the woods. The first time I met Errol, I'd needed to get away from my folks. I got so much more than an escape when I stumbled upon him in the trees that separated our parents' properties. Errol was the best friend I could imagine having as a teenager.

Back then, I didn't have words for the way I felt when my father called me his little princess. Or when my mother bought my first training bra when I was thirteen and gave it to me like it was supposed to be this wonderful rite of passage. She wanted it to be this big moment between us. We had a moment, but not the sort she'd intended.

That day, Mom came home with back to school clothes. All of them hyper-feminine. Her speech about our latest move being the perfect time to, 'put my tomboy phase behind me,' felt like a gut punch.

I lost my shit about it, screaming that hockey players

don't wear skirts or dresses or pink. They can. I know plenty who do. But *I* didn't want to. We got into a screaming match and my father got involved.

Dad was already three beers deep with no plans of stopping, even though it was barely past noon. I ran before he could grab me. He didn't chase me once I cleared the old screen door. His heavy stomping steps, hard on my heels, halted abruptly as the screen slammed closed with a loud metallic bang. My father's furious shouting was the only thing that followed me into the trees behind our new place.

Now I know the word. Dysphoria. All I knew then, was that if I could have run away from my own skin, I'd have done it. Hockey had been my escape, but the rink hadn't been an option that midsummer day, not long after we moved to BC, so I'd run into the woods and found Errol.

He was trying to build something sheltered amongst a thick stand of evergreens with scrap wood scavenged from his father's work sites. I watched him from behind a scrubby tree until he nearly beaned himself trying to nail a board between two poorly erected posts. That was when I jumped in to help him.

I startled him into dropping his hammer on his foot. He cursed and hopped around, and I couldn't help laughing. That moment of hilarity was like a dam bursting inside me. I erupted into hysterics, all the pent up emotion flowing out of me.

Errol scowled at me at first, unimpressed that I was laughing at his injury. He pursed his lips, all prim and uptight. His expression made me laugh harder, gasping for breath as tears leaked from my eyes. Those tears were safe to cry, I could let myself laugh. Errol pushed his thick black-rimmed glasses up his long nose. "Are you finished?"

"No, sorry. It's just..." I tried to explain what was so funny, that I wasn't laughing *at* him, not really. The words kept getting lost in more laughter, though. When I wiped at the tears, my sleeve rode up my arm and he saw the fading greenish marks on my wrist. He didn't seem so annoyed anymore. He grabbed at my hand and shoved up my sleeve.

"Hockey," I lied. Not entirely a lie, I justified it. A lot of my bruises *were* from hockey.

Errol gave me a skeptical glance. "You play hockey in the summer?"

"Yeah, indoor rinks are open year round," I told him with a superior grin.

"Not around here," Errol said.

"I'm not from around here," I shot back. Mom had to drive me the hour into Kelowna for practice, or I had to carpool with teammates or take a long bus ride to get to the rink. Totally worth it for ice time.

"I'm Errol. Who are you?" He held out a hand, and we shook, the sort of firm, confident gesture my dad would have called manly.

"Rene. Pronounced like that, spelled R-E-N-E. And don't call me a girl." I jutted out my chin in challenge, a lifetime of experience telling me to expect a fight.

"Okay." Errol looked me up and down. "Are you a boy, then?"

"No."

"Okay." He shrugged.

I narrowed my eyes at him. "You don't want to ask anything else?"

Errol shrugged again. "So, you're just Rene, right?"

"Yeah, just Rene," I said, wary and relieved in equal

measure. That was exactly what I wanted, and I didn't trust his ready acceptance not to have a catch, but I wanted this. "I think we could be friends, Errol."

"Well, if you want to be friends, why don't you hold that board for me and we can build this fort together." Errol gestured at the board he'd dropped with his hammer.

"Is that what you're trying to build? It sort of looks like a heap of wood and tetanus waiting to happen," I said, cocking my head to examine his not so stellar construction efforts up close.

Errol scowled. We tried to erect the walls of the fort he envisioned with little luck. I didn't tell him we were too old for tree forts. He didn't treat me like a freak. Errol invited me home for dinner around suppertime. I went, because, after the fight and running away, I knew there wasn't a meal waiting for me at my house. Afterward, I snuck home from Errol's for the first time. It was far from the last.

We eventually got his dad's help to build a structurally sound fort in the woods. I had a moment of panicked horror when I mentioned the project in front of Errol's father before I realized that Errol hadn't told his dad about the project. Nor had he asked permission to use his tools and scrap wood.

My fear that Mr. Dawes would be mad or punish Errol must have been obvious to everyone at the table. My dad would have been livid if I'd done something similar. Mr. Dawes didn't get mad, just offered his help in his soft, even voice. Errol kicked my foot under the table to get my attention and flashed me a reassuring smile. Mrs. Dawes got us both enormous bowls of ice cream for dessert. She used to fuss over me like she thought I was wasting away.

The next weekend we had an actual building plan, and the fort came together fast with the three of us working with the proper materials and tools. That ramshackle fort was the second place I ever felt like I could be myself. The ice where I was just a hockey player and the tree fort where I was just Rene.

Only, it wasn't the four walls that defined the space; it was Errol. He gave me room to be myself, even before either of us figured out who that was. Later, I returned the favor, giving him the space to figure out his sexuality and room to shape our relationship so that it met both our needs.

My parents don't live there anymore. They haven't for a few years. Dad's drinking caught up with his liver and he's got cirrhosis. Mom moved him to Kelowna to a retirement community where she can hire a home health aid to assist with taking care of him.

They stopped sending me money around the same time. They needed it for Dad's nursing care. Plus, Mom made it clear playing hockey wasn't a real career choice and playing at being a boy wasn't a real life choice. Fuck my parents. I sigh, and Errol gives me a concerned glance.

"You okay?" he asks, rubbing his thumb over the back of my hand.

"Yeah. Just thinking."

"About?" he prompts.

"The day we met."

"You laughed at me," Errol recalls.

"No one makes me laugh like you do, stud." I poke his side.

"Glad you think my lack of any carpentry skills is so hilarious," Errol says, sounding amused.

"I needed that laugh so bad."

"I know." Errol sobers. He glances at Mo in the rear-view, checking that he's still asleep before he says, "We never talk about it, but I know he hit you. I wish I'd done something to stop it."

I'd known he figured it out. He'd tried to bring it up when we were kids, but I always shot him down and changed the subject.

I shrug. "What could you have done? You were a kid, too. It wasn't like it was constant, I got good at avoiding him. Besides, anytime anyone reported anything we moved. I had a couple of coaches and teachers over the years who figured it out. Nothing ever stuck. There was always a cover story, and I got a lot of bruises and broken bones playing hockey. You were what kept me going, Errol. I didn't want to move again."

"Still."

"You did what you could." I rest my hand on his thigh, and he turns it to twine our fingers together. "Even after you went away to university, your folks fed me and gave me a place to sleep if it got too bad at home. Anyway, I don't want my parents to get so much as a glance at Mo. Not ever."

"They won't," he promises. "They left the area and my folks agreed to keep Mo off their social media."

"Okay."

"My folks always cared about you, Rene. They'll get over their hurt if we give them time." Errol's still holding my left hand, squeezing gently to remind me he's got my back. I sit on my right hand to keep from chewing the nails again.

"I really am sorry," I say.

"You've got to stop apologizing, imzadi. We made Mo

together. I'm sorry you ever felt like you couldn't share that with me. It breaks my heart that you felt like you had to take that all on yourself. Yeah, I was mad when you told me, but I'm also mad at myself for not being there to support you. For letting you walk out of my life because what you said hurt me. I know you, Rene, I should have known you needed me."

"No more apologies?" I suggest with a wry chuckle.

"No more apologies," Errol says. "How about we play some music?"

"Sounds good," I agree. He lets me pick the radio station, but the options are limited and reception is crap. We both sing along to the upbeat pop music that crackles out of the speakers all the way to his parent's town anyway.

CHAPTER 18

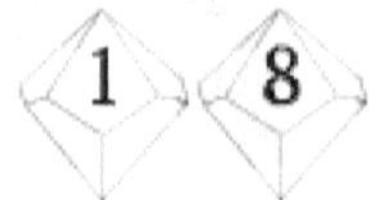

Errol

Mo wakes up when I stop in town to gas up the car. I watch him in the rearview mirror. He stretches his arms and looks around himself, still seeming bleary-eyed from his nap. "Are we there?" he asks through a yawn.

"Almost, bud," Rene says, turning in their seat to smile at him.

"And I'm going to meet Grandma and Grandpa?" he asks, fiddling with his booster seat's straps.

"That's right," I say. "My mom and dad are so excited to meet you, Mo."

"What if they don't like me?" Mo asks.

"They'll love you, Momo," Rene says.

"They will," I agree.

Mo kicks his legs, thinking for a minute. Then he asks, "What about Papa's parents?"

"They're not kind people, Mo, remember?" Rene says.

"So, I'm not meeting them, too?" Mo asks.

"No, you're not," I say, giving Rene's hand a squeeze.

"Okay." Mo drops it and we get back on the road. This last stretch is familiar, no matter how many years have passed since I called this place home.

Rene chews on their nails as we turn up the long gravel driveway to my childhood home. Mo has either picked up on his papa's nerves or he's still sleepy because he doesn't say a word as he watches the passing scenery.

As soon as I put the car into park behind Mom's old Jeep, the front door of the house bursts open and both my parents come out to greet us. Rene clutches my hand like a lifeline.

"This visit will be fine," I say. Rene releases their grip on my hand to chew their nails. I sigh and gently tug their hand away from their mouth.

"I'll be right by your side, imzadi," I say. For good measure, I lean over and give them a chaste kiss. Rene takes a moment to relax into it, no doubt conscious of my parents watching us. That's part of why I did it. My folks might need the reminder that Rene is my person and that isn't changing, no matter what they think of our relationship. I caress Rene's cheek, then adjust my glasses and turn to unbuckle Mo just as my mother opens his door and holds out her arms for a hug.

"Oh, look at you! Would you like to give your grandma a hug, dear?" Mom restrains herself short of scooping Mo out of his seat.

Mo glances to Rene and I, questioning and nervous.

"Mom, this is Monet. Mo, this is your grandmother. You don't have to hug her, if you aren't comfortable with that, yet." I introduce them, giving Mom a warning look not to frighten the kid. We talked about giving him space when I called to confirm our visit.

"Oh, my heavens! Monet, you look just like your daddy did at your age, so tall, come and let us have a look at you! Errol, get out here and give your mother a hug," she demands.

It's obvious I'm not the Dawes boy she wants to be hugging the most right now, but I get out and circle around the car to hug her. Mom squeezes the breath out of my lungs and rocks me from side to side. It's been a while since my last visit and I feel a bit guilty about that. I get busy with work and my friends, and it's easy to forget my parents won't be here forever.

My father embraces me, too. Rene helps Mo out of the car and our kid clings to their neck, long legs wrapped around his papa when my folks finish greeting me.

"Good to see you again, Rene," Dad offers Rene a handshake and Rene juggles Mo onto one hip to oblige him.

"Yeah, you too, Mr. Dawes," they say awkwardly.

"Please, you can call me Charles, or Dad. How have you been? Busy, I'm sure. There's nothing like a little one to keep you on your toes." Dad looks like it's killing him not to touch Mo. He keeps his hands to himself as he talks to Rene. "And you, young man, can call me Gramps, or Grandpa, or anything else you like. Your daddy tells us you like cars?"

Mo nods shyly.

"Well, then I think you're going to love what your grandma picked out for your room, would you like to take my hand and I can show you?"

Mo considers, then nods. Rene lowers him to the ground, and Mo takes my dad's hand to go with him. Rene and I follow right behind, shooing the kid along when he glances back at us. He forgets his reticence when Dad opens the door to what used to be my bedroom and reveals that a toy store exploded in there since my last visit.

Alongside what can only be every toy with wheels on the market, there is also an overflowing toy chest. A shelf stuffed full of picture books stands beside a twin bed with race car bedding. The large area rug has little buildings and roads printed on it for him to drive the cars along.

"Wow!" Mo exclaims. "Can I play with your toys, Gramps?"

"You sure can, they're all for you, kiddo," Dad says.

"Thanks!" Mo gives his leg a quick hug, then goes for the remote control monster truck. Soon, he's got my dad helping him drive it around the room like an old pro. Mom hovers near the door. Rene clutches my hand, glued to my side.

"You alright playing in here with Grandpa while Papa and I bring in our bags, Mo?" I ask after a moment has passed.

"Okay," Mo agrees, distracted by backing the big truck over a smaller car.

Rene and I turn to go back outside to grab our bags. Mom stays in the doorway, watching Mo with eyes that glisten with unshed tears. I squeeze her shoulder and she tears her eyes away from him to meet my gaze.

"He'll warm up to you, give him time, Mom," I say, because I know how she feels. Cheated out of her place in Mo's life. I went through the same sense of loss not two weeks ago. But this isn't about us, we're the adults, and Mo needs to know we'll respect his boundaries more than we need to hug him.

"You two made a beautiful kid." Mom pats my cheek as

I squeeze past her. She still doesn't speak to Rene. From their closed posture and anxious glances, it's clear Rene is acutely aware of the non-greeting from my mother.

"Rene's done an amazing job raising him," I say.

Mom flinches.

"Are we in the guest room?" I ask.

"Yes, across the hall," Mom points, as if they might have moved the spare room since I last visited.

"Thanks," I kiss Mom's cheek and take Rene's hand to go back for our bags.

Unfortunately, Mom doesn't take the hint to give Rene and me a minute alone. Instead of pining over Mo from the doorway, Mom follows us back out to the car.

"He won't want to leave," Rene jokes weakly as I open the trunk.

"My grandson is welcome here, anytime. Maybe we can watch him for you, over the summer."

"We already have childcare arranged, but thanks for the offer, Mom," I say through gritted teeth. Mo doesn't need any more upheaval.

"You mentioned that, I want to help you though," Mom says.

"When he's more comfortable with you and Dad, Rene and I can discuss extended visits. For now, he's going through some major changes. I don't think it's a good idea to throw too much at him at once. We weren't even sure whether this visit was a great idea, so don't make us regret coming," I say.

Mom looks upset, but she nods. "Fine. What would you like for dinner? Any dietary restrictions? I have cookie dough ready to bake. Do you think he'll like my lemon squares? I made a batch last night."

"You did?" Rene asks, and they seem stunned by that

tidbit. Mom sighs and finally turns to face Rene, acknowledging them directly for the first time.

"Yes, dear. I remember how you used to gorge yourself on my lemon squares." Mom holds out her hands and Rene closes the distance. Mom gives Rene a hug and then pats Rene's cheek the way she did when we were kids. "I can be mad at the choices you made and still care about you, dear. If Errol can forgive you, then I will too. Give me time?"

"Yeah, okay, Mrs. Dawes."

"Mona, or Mom, dear. My son says you're his person, that makes you ours, alright?"

"Alright, Mona," Rene says awkwardly. I hand Rene Mo's backpack and his favorite Ollie Owl action figure, then I grab both suitcases and lug them into the house. Mom offers us beverages, then goes off to the kitchen to get them. Rene brings Mo's things to his room for the night. I put our suitcase in our room then drag his bag into the bedroom where Mo and my dad have moved on to racing slot cars around a track.

Rene's sitting on the edge of the bed, watching as Mo exclaims over all the toys. They flash me a wan smile when I join them, sitting on the bed and watching Mo bond with my dad.

Mom joins us with a tray of coffee, cookies, and juice for Mo. It's early enough in the day that I don't think twice about the coffee. Rene hesitates before having a cup, heavy on the flavored creamer.

The plate of lemon squares is enough to tear Mo away from his new toys.

Mom beams at him when he tries a nibble of his treat, and grabs for a second helping. Rene moans at the taste, then looks embarrassed about it.

"These are so good," Mo declares, overshadowing any attention on Rene. "Thanks, Grandma," he adds, crumbs falling out of his mouth when he flashes her a gap-toothed grin. The title is tentative. Something he's saying because he realizes the adults in the room want to hear it. The same stilted way he said Daddy for the first week living with me. Now it sounds more natural, like it's really who I am to him.

I don't doubt Grandma and Gramps will flow more easily too, if they keep giving him room. Honestly, I expected to have to remind them to back off, but my folks are following the guidelines we set out for them before the visit. Much as I know it's killing them, they are respecting Mo's space and boundaries. This meeting is going well. Better than I expected, even.

Mom beams at Mo as she offers to make another batch. "These were your papa's favorites when they were growing up," she says with genuine fondness, and they both glance at Rene.

"Still are," Rene agrees, taking another bite of their treat.

"What was Daddy's favorite?" Mo asks.

"Chocolate chip," Rene, Mom, and I all say at the same time. Mo laughs.

"Can we have those too?" he asks.

"Honey, Grandma will make any cookies your little heart desires, all you have to do is ask," Mom says.

"Even Christmas cookies?" Mo checks.

"Even Christmas cookies," Mom agrees with a smile.

"What about Hanukkah cookies?" Mo asks, brow furrowed. "For Uncle Emil."

"Sure, those too," Mom agrees. She met Emil when she visited me around Christmas last year. Insisted on bringing over dinner for my friends who had a new baby. "I'm sure baby Rain will want to share your cookies soon."

Mo makes a face. "Babies can't have solid food yet, Grandma. They only drink milk and eat squishy baby food."

"Is that so?" Mom asks, an amused glint in her eyes.

"Yeah. I know all about babies, I'm a big helper with Rain and Otis. If I keep being responsible, then Papa and Daddy might get me a dog for my birthday."

"We'll see about that, Momo, don't push," Rene chides him. Mo shoots us an apologetic look.

"Do you have a dog, Grandma?" he asks, perking up as though the idea just occurred to him.

"No, we've got a cat lurking around here somewhere, though," Dad says.

"What's the cat's name?" Mo asks, glancing around the room like the animal might burst out of hiding.

"Mouse."

Mo giggles. "That's a silly name for a cat."

Mom smiles at his amusement. "If you'd like to meet her, we can go to the kitchen and get out her treats and I bet you she'll come to investigate."

"Yes!" Mo agrees. He hops up and takes Mom's hand, much to her delight, and they go to summon the cat. Mouse is a sucker for the sound of a tuna tin opening, doubtless the cat will appear. It's a good bonding moment for Mom and Mo. Rene and I stay put, eating our snack while Dad gets creakily to his feet. Rene sets aside their untouched coffee.

"These old bones are getting too stiff to play on the floor," he says ruefully as he moves to sit in an old armchair placed by the bookshelf. "I'm glad all three of you could make it this weekend. Rene, how have you been, dear?"

Rene looks like a deer in the headlights at the question. Dad's entire demeanor softens when he talks to them, like he's afraid of spooking them. My dad was always a gentle man. Never more so than when Rene visited. That hasn't changed. I think he had an inkling what their home life was like before I did. From that first tense dinner, when they got that frozen terrified expression over his reaction to my sneaking his tools into the woods. Rene was always welcome in our home, always safe there.

"We're adjusting to the move. Started coaching hockey, and that's going well. It's a bit of a dream job, honestly."

"That's wonderful, I know how much you loved being on the ice." Dad beams at Rene.

"Yeah, it's pretty great. Right now, we're running summer camps with younger kids."

"They're taking Mo next week," I interject, patting Rene's thigh. "I'm nervous to see him on the ice." That's an understatement, there's a reason people believed Rene when they blamed all their injuries on their sport. I remember the one concussion Rene got on the ice as a teenager with vivid clarity. There's no way my heart can take watching Mo get hurt.

"I love that you're worried about him, you old mother hen, but he's been skating since he could walk." Rene flashes me an apologetic smile for the reminder of everything I've missed. Those moments are starting to sting less, now that I'm getting the chance to make new memories with Mo. "Besides, peewee summer camp isn't the same as the juniors. We mostly practice skating drills. And we ref the crap out of their scrimmages each session.

You're welcome to watch with the other parents at pick up time."

"I'll be there. Maybe we can have dinner out afterward, as a family."

"I'm sure Mo would love that," Rene says.

Dad looks between the two of us with fondness.

"I'm sure Mo is excited to share his papa's love of the game," Dad says. "Are you glad to be back in BC, Rene?"

"Yeah." Rene turns to glance at me, a soft smile warming their expression. "It's good. Definitely made the right move." They lay a hand on my knee, and I'm pretty sure they mean more than just coming back to the province.

CHAPTER 19

Rene

In hindsight, I should have seen this coming. Something was bound to fuck up the perfect little life I'd stumbled into when I moved into Errol's home. I'd moved enough as a kid to realize that upending our lives and bringing new people into Mo's world had to be hard on him. No matter how doting and lovely all the new people act, it's a lot.

I took every precaution possible to give him consistency. I'd paid exorbitant fees to ship as much of his clothing, toys, and his worn but familiar bedding as I could to our new place.

We've worked out ways for him to stay in touch with his best friend, Laurent. They video chat a few times a week and play games together on the Switch almost daily since swapping friend codes.

Still, he has a new school, a new home, new rules, a new dad and extended family. Even the language is less familiar. He only knows English at all because we spoke both French and English at home. A part of me always longed to move home. Teaching my son the language I grew up with let me cling to that glimmer of hope that there *was* a home for me to return to. The secret hope I'd buried too deep to acknowledge even to myself, was that dream of home always included Errol.

I don't regret the decision to return, but it means everything in Mo's life has changed. Objectively, none of those changes are for the worse. Living here means I can give Mo a better life. But it's still a drastic change, and that's hard for anyone.

The problems start with him shaking me awake in the middle of the night when we're staying with Errol's folks. At first, I think it's just fear of an unfamiliar place, but his cheeks are wet with tears when he tells me he peed his bed. The kid looks mortified, so I take him back to his room, help him clean up and change his PJs and the sheets.

We left behind middle-of-the-night accidents ages ago. Mo's been out of pull-ups since he decided, aged three, that diapers were for babies and he was a big boy now. He's had accidents here and there over the years, but it's been years since we resorted to layered waterproof mattress covers in case of multiple accidents in a night.

After the second accident in as many hours, I'm too exhausted to deal with another sheet change. His bladder has to be empty now, so I just clean him up and tuck him into our bed with a towel under him, just in case. Errol wakes up when we're crawling back under the covers.

"What's wrong?" he asks, reaching for his glasses.

"Nothing. Mo's sleeping with us," I say. Errol leaves his glasses on the nightstand and rolls over to spoon me against his body. He kisses the nape of my neck and pats Mo's back.

"Night," Errol mumbles, not prying into why Mo is joining us at three in the morning.

I relax. Mo sleeps until morning without another incident. The rest of our visit and the drive home are uneventful. Then we repeat the whole rigamarole the next night at home, leaving him exhausted for his first day of hockey camp.

I pick up some pull-ups for Monday night. Mo is not happy about that and he has his first major blow-up in front of Errol. A massive, throwing himself on the floor screaming, tantrum. To his credit, Errol handles it well. He keeps his cool and calmly repeats that Mo needs to wear the pull-ups to bed if he wants a bedtime story. Mo chucks the book across the room.

The kid just doesn't have the spoons to cope. We say goodnight and give him his space. Mo strips his bedding into a blanket nest on the floor and falls asleep there. It isn't even a surprise when he stumbles into our bed in the wee hours. He put on his pull-up before joining us, so I count it as a victory.

The tantrums over everything pick up steam from there. Silver lining, it probably means he is becoming comfortable in our new home, now that he feels secure enough to act out. That's not much of a comfort when he's losing his shit on the regular, and I don't know how to help him. He makes Errol and I late to work three days running by refusing to eat his breakfast and dawdling over his clothing instead of getting dressed. Again, Errol takes it in stride and he doesn't take out his frustration with Mo. At least the kid behaves himself at hockey camp, although he gets grumpy if I try to tell him anything about improving his form on the ice. I let my coworkers direct him, if he needs correction. He makes friends with the other kids, two of whom attend his new school.

We cave and just feed the kid a granola bar in the car on the way to the rink on Friday. Then that's the only thing he wants for breakfast all weekend, but at least he eats healthy food during the day. I try not to feel too guilty over the sugary breakfast replacement. The next week he refuses to eat even the granola bars for us, though Emil reports that he eats his healthy snacks and lunch. At least Mo's better behaved during the day, walking Otis and eager to help take care of Rain.

By the start of my fourth week at work, and his first week at the new school, the acting out at home is getting unbearable though, and I'm regretting all my life choices. Not on a personal level. My job is amazing, the best I've ever had. I love working with the rest of the coaching staff and being back on the ice. Even just running skating drills with little kids who still wobble on their skates is fulfilling.

Errol is everything I remember him being. Everything I could desire in a partner. He set the bar so high when we were young that none of the casual dates I tried in Montreal stood a chance of being something more. They couldn't hold a candle to my first love. The boy I met in the woods, who made me laugh at a moment I needed the catharsis so bad I thought I might burst. Errol has always been there for me. Supportive and understanding like no other. That hasn't changed, and it's a miracle he's let me back into his life. I'm not about to look a gift horse in the mouth.

No, I never dared to hope those aspects of my life

could be this perfect. Except that none of that good stuff matters when Mo is miserable. When he sobs that he misses home. He asks about our old car, his old teacher, our friends. Even the too-small shit hole apartment with neighbors who kept him up at night with their screaming fights. It's ridiculous.

The school gets him set up for the early French immersion track, so his classes will still be in French. The language he's most used to, though the longer we're here the less he defaults to French, even when he's exhausted from all the nighttime waking.

I'm exhausted too. And frustrated from dealing with Mo's millionth tantrum of the day. And heartbroken that he's struggling and I can't make it better.

It's bedtime on the Sunday night before he's registered to start grade one when I finally give up even trying to be civil. I snap at Mo that he needs to shut off his game, get his butt in his pull-ups, and then into bed. He loses it. His face just crumples. I know it's the impotent rage of a frustrated, overtired kid talking when he screams that he hates me. That he wishes I wasn't his papa. Those words are still a gut punch.

Mo screams that he wants to move in with Laurent. Then he'd have the brother and sister he so desperately wants and a mom and dad who love him. I can't even respond to his anger, it's all too much. That's when Errol steps in to defuse the situation.

Something about him intervening just throws me back. Back to screaming arguments between me and my mother. The both of us flinching at the heavy stomping footsteps bearing down on us. The way my body always froze up like a startled rabbit as my father's powerful hands grabbed me with bruising strength. His boozy breath in my face as he forced me to look him in the eye. His harsh, angry voice demanding respect he'd never earned.

There's no stomping or yelling in my present reality. No threats or violence. Just an irate six-year-old crying on the sofa and Errol murmuring soothing words, urging him to go to his room and cool off before he says anything else he'll regret. I'm aware that this is nothing like that momentary flashback. Errol is nothing like my father. I still flinch when Errol's fingers brush my arm to ask if I'm alright. I'm not, so I just shake my head. He goes to pull back, but I can't stand the thought of him thinking I'm rejecting him. I grab for his arm, clinging to him like a lifeline.

Errol doesn't speak while I sob into his shoulder. He just holds me and rocks me until all the emotion and remembered terror has poured out of me and I'm drained dry.

"Want to talk about it?" Errol asks when I finally pull out of his embrace.

I shrug.

"That wasn't just about what Mo said," Errol observes.

"No," I admit, scrubbing the tears from my face.

"I think," Errol says, then he shakes his head and rubs his temples. "No, I don't think. I know we need some professional help with this. We've got a metric shit-ton of baggage between the three of us. Mo shouldn't have to shoulder that, but it's there. I think talking to a counselor might help him process all the changes in his life. Gregor can hook us up with names for LGBTQ2+ friendly services, that's a huge part of his job, so he knows what's available. But we should book an appointment for Mo at least."

"You saying you think I screwed up our kid or that I need my head shrunk?" I joke weakly through a sniffle. Considering I just had a snot-faced breakdown all over him, it's not an unfair assumption.

Errol shakes his head and gives me a fondly exasperated look. "I didn't say that. You are an amazing parent. I think we all need to process everything, though. As a family and as individuals. There's a reason we keep apologizing to each other over our past. I suspect a huge part of that is we haven't dealt with the gaping wounds it left behind. You most of all, Rene. You don't have to talk about what your family was like with me. I understand you have triggers, but I think it would benefit you to talk about it."

I can't deny he's right. He was here for that ridiculous flashback. "I didn't really think you were him."

"I know," Errol strokes my cheek. His touch tethers me to reality. I grab his hand and keep it pressed against my face, turning to kiss his palm.

"I know you'd never hurt me. Either of us," I say with utter conviction.

"Can you tell me what just happened?" he asks. I sigh. It's difficult to talk about, and few people have cared enough to ask. The last time I tried opening up about my past, I almost fucked everything up. Except this is Errol; I can tell him anything. So I do.

CHAPTER 20

2 0

Errol

"When you put yourself between us, it just reminded me of fighting with my mom. My brain got tripped up remembering." Rene shrugs and I can fill in the blanks.

"He hit you," I bring up the seldom mentioned truth about their family. I expect them to deflect like they always do, but it seems like they need to lance those old wounds before they fester any longer.

"Yeah," Rene admits, shoulders slumping. They pick at their cuticles and refuse to meet my eyes, but they don't change the subject or brush it off, for once. "Mostly when he was drunk. If he hit mom too, it was never in front of me. I learned to avoid him, and spend most of my time at school, or the rink, or with friends. Only went home when it was unavoidable."

"And you never saw someone about it?" I ask. "I mean, afterward. You already explained why you didn't make waves before leaving home."

"I tried. Once." Rene blows out a frustrated breath. I can see the irritation in their expressive face as they explain. "They make you get counseling before they'll do surgery. Like I need some shrink's permission to be me. It's bullshit gatekeeping awfulness, but that's the medical guidelines, because god forbid we let trans people have bodily autonomy. And, yeah, not every therapist uses it to police gender, but that's what it feels like. So I had to get a note agreeing that I'm trans. I was a naïve idiot the first time I went. Told the counselor everything. How Dad used to knock me around and I'm nonbinary, not a trans man. He decided I was using my gender identity to hide from my trauma. Refused to write me the letter I needed to yeet the teat. So I waited months for an appointment with a different counselor and paid out of pocket for a few therapy sessions, and I lied. Told them I was a binary trans man and glossed over the abuse. That convinced them to write my referral letter. I had to repeat the same lines later to get two letters of permission signing off on my metoidioplasty." They huff a humorless laugh. "Anyone who tells you they're worried about trans kids getting irreversible procedures without being sure of who they are has obviously never tried to access trans related healthcare. It sucks, never being sure if my doctors will take me seriously or deny me care."

"That's..." I shake my head, trailing off on a low whistle.

"It's fucking awful," Rene fills in the blank with a sharp nod, voice close to breaking with the remembered bitterness. "It was so awful. I hate pretending to be someone I'm not, even if it's just telling a counselor I'm a man. It's close enough to the truth, but it still makes me cringe to say it. Just because it's less wrong for me than being seen as a woman..." they shake their head and blow out a noisy frustrated breath. "Sorry, you don't need me emotionally vomiting all over you. It's been a long couple weeks."

"Seems like you've had rough *years*, Rene. Not just weeks," I say. Then I slowly lift my arm toward them in invitation, letting Rene step into my side and wrapping my arm around their shoulders.

"Yeah. That too," Rene agrees, leaning into my touch.

"You can always talk to me," I murmur.

"Okay." Rene sighs, resting their head on my shoulder and closing their weary eyes. "Is it okay if we don't? My point was, it's ingrained that if I talk about this stuff, it gets used against me. As a kid, I mentioned it to a teacher. My folks pulled me out of school and we moved across the province. Once a hockey coach noticed bruises, and I almost lost all my access to the ice, the one place I could be myself. I spilled my guts to the first counselor I saw. He almost prevented my transition. I just..." Rene trails off, shaking their head. When they continue, their voice sounds weak, defeated. "I've never had much that's been mine in life, Errol. Hockey and Mo. And maybe you? I don't want to lose that over bullshit that shouldn't matter anymore. It's over, and I don't want it to take away anything else."

"That's fair, Rene. More than fair," I say, I have no right to pry at their wounds. "I still think we should try counseling. If you don't feel comfortable talking about that stuff yet, that's fine. We can all learn healthy ways to cope with stress and how to support you when something reminds you of the past. I know you were out of it, but whatever happened, when you shut down, it scared Mo,"

I say. It's absolutely playing dirty, but the kid busted out sobbing when Rene had what must have been a flashback, however brief it may have been. This episode made it pretty clear that Rene needs help. And if they won't take care of themself for their own sake, I know without a doubt that they'll do it for Mo's sake.

"I scared him?" Rene asks.

"He's ok now. I bet he already fell asleep," I reassure them.

Rene nods stiffly. "Okay. Book the appointments, I guess. I can't promise it will help, but ignoring it sure hasn't done me any favors. It's not like they can take back my dick now that I've had my surgeries."

It's a weak joke, but I chuckle along with them. They tip toward the hysterical and they hug me a little too tight, but I think we're in an alright place. On the path toward healing from our past hurts.

When we check on Mo, he's asleep in a tangle of blankets in the middle of his floor. Rene kisses him on the forehead and stares at him for ages before taking my hand and leading me to our bed.

We lie awake for a long time. Rene traces their fingers over my face as if they want to memorize it. When they kiss me, it's gentle, seeking connection more than anything sexual.

"I love you, Errol," they murmur against my lips.

"I love you too, Rene. To the moon and back. Now sleep, I've got you, imzadi" I give them a final chaste kiss, then another on their forehead and Rene turns to snuggle their back to my front. It feels right to have them in my arms.

When Mo joins us, just before dawn, he crawls in on my side instead of Rene's for once. It could be because they had a fight last night, but I choose to believe it's that he is warming up to me as his second parent. Whatever the reason, I adjust to snuggle him close and Rene rolls in their sleep to throw an arm around us both.

CHAPTER 21

Rene

I had my doubts about this Saturday appointment from the moment Errol told me about it. Gregor pulled strings for us to see a therapist he works with on short-notice. Marge Applebaum's reception area is nothing inspiring. Shabby industrial carpets and crappy hard plastic waiting room chairs. Old magazines with frayed covers lay scattered across the mismatched end tables. Framed motivational posters adorn the walls. No one is working reception on the weekend, so we're the only ones in the room as we wait.

Mo gravitates to the truck sitting atop the magazines, driving it around the room noisily no matter how many times I remind him to keep the noise down. Errol takes my hand and squeezes it when it drifts toward my mouth.

My nerves have me on edge. We got a bunch of intake paperwork to fill out along with the appointment confirmation. I fuss with the stack of papers while we wait. The questions on the intake forms asked about why we booked our appointments and detailed basic background on all of us. Even writing out why I'm here made my stomach churn with nerves.

The message said Marge wants all three of us present for Mo's appointment to address his behavior issues relating to the move. Then Errol has plans to take Mo for ice cream to keep him occupied while I endure my turn in the hot seat.

Marge comes to get us when it's time. She introduces herself, all bright smiles and soft words that have Mo engaging with her. His eyes widen at the array of toys in her office, and he immediately gravitates toward a lifelike baby doll. He grabs it and spends most of the appointment playing with it while we talk. Marge asks him all about the changes in our family over the past month and how it's made him feel.

As Mo answers the gently probing questions, I can't help thinking the kid would make a phenomenal big brother. There's even a small part of me that wants to give him the sibling he so longs for. An even bigger part of me wants to give all those missed experiences to Errol. Give myself the chance to do all the parenting milestones with Errol at my side. It wouldn't be the same traumatic experience here that my unplanned teenage pregnancy with Mo had been.

On an intellectual level, I know that having a supportive partner and going to a queer friendly practice for prenatal care would take care of most of my issues. But my pregnancy with Mo destroyed my mental health and I'm in no place to be even considering going through even a fraction of that hell again. Still. I can't shake the thought that it would be different. Better. Something I might even deserve to enjoy experiencing with the man I love at my side.

That's not what today is about. Another change is the last thing our son needs while he's struggling. Least of all one he might perceive as a do-over with a replacement kid. A baby to take away attention and love when he's already insecure will only make this worse, right?

Another thing to discuss when it's my turn with the shrink. Or if this goes well, I might risk broaching the subject at a later appointment.

Mo seems unperturbed by the entire session. To all appearances, he's just playing with toys and talking to the gray-haired woman with deep laugh lines that crinkle around her eyes when she smiles. She doesn't look like someone who wants to stand between me and what I need to be happy and whole. The therapists I saw in Montreal hadn't looked like they would be the gatekeepers who determined my fate either, though.

The family appointment ends with Marge chatting more directly with Errol and me. Mo sits and plays with toy dinosaurs, the doll tucked in for a nap nearby. Nothing she says is unexpected. Mo's adjusting to some big changes in his life. It's normal for him to act out or experience regressions, like wetting the bed. He'll adjust and get back to himself, and we just need to remain patient with him. It's what I expected, but I find myself reassured more than I'd have guessed to hear that what he's going through is normal. This professional doesn't think I completely fucked up my kid with my shitty life choices.

We conclude the session with Marge, going over a couple of breathing exercises with all of us for Mo to use when he gets overwhelmed. That way, he can try to get calm instead of melting down. It's kind of adorable watching him meditate. His serious face reminds me so much of Errol in that moment.

The appointment ends and Errol takes Mo's hand. They leave for their ice cream outing while I get my head shrunk. Mo seems happy enough to go with his daddy. I wave and tell them to have fun, and then I brace myself for what comes next. The toys remain strewn across the low table where Mo left them.

"What, other than your concern about your son, brings you to me today, Rene?" Marge asks, her tone all friendly neutrality. Her words jerk my attention away from the abandoned toys.

I pull a throw pillow into my lap to keep my hands occupied. I glance around the room, taking it all in again. Miniature pride flags stick out of a cup of pens. Not just the rainbow one either. The trans flag is there, too.

Gregor wouldn't have sent us to anyone who didn't have experience with queer clients. It still lets me breathe easier that she wants to advertise this is a safe space. Despite that, I can't quite find the words to break the silence that stretches after Mo and Errol leave. I shake my head.

"I take it from your intake forms that you had a reason beyond reconciling with your son's other father for booking this appointment with me?" Marge prompts me.

"Oh, uh, yeah," I say, glancing at her, and then away again to study the framed quote on the wall past her shoulder.

"Care to share what that reason might be?" she asks. The words are almost harsh, but the way she says them softens the question. I don't think I can handle this. Heat seems to rise through my body, like I might catch fire if I have to sit here and do this. Focus on the past. Rip open old wounds for her to examine them.

"No." I squirm in my seat.

She gives me an indulgent look. "Alright, no pressure. Why don't you tell me what made you decide to come in today?"

"Isn't that the same question?" I scowl at her.

She gives me a soft smile. "Not quite. What was it about your life that made you decide you needed to talk to a therapist?"

"Uh, everything?" I gesture toward the closed door that Mo just left through. "I fucked up everything. And now it feels like I even ruined the one thing I thought I was decent at, being Mo's papa. He's having a hard time, and it's my fault for being stupid and hiding him and for uprooting his life and bringing him back here."

"You did the very best you could, Rene. You need to cut some slack to the scared teenager who made the best choices they could with no support system to speak of," she says. Her tone makes it clear there's no room for contradicting her. I sit there, squeezing the pillow and absorbing the unadorned truth in her words.

"I did the best I could," I repeat.

"That's right." She nods. "And from my session with your son, the results speak for themselves. He's struggling with the move, like any six-year-old would. But the boy I just met is kind and nurturing. He is secure knowing that he is loved and wanted at home. The fact he's been acting out is a sign that he knows he's safe with you and his other father. That's a good thing, even if it doesn't feel like that when he's having a meltdown over bedtime."

She flashes me a small conspiratorial grin and I force myself to return the expression. It's a relief to hear a neutral party tell me I didn't fuck up my kid any more than any other parent. "Right now, we're here to talk about you and your needs."

"I need to be the parent he deserves," I say, smoothing my thumb along the pillow's edge.

"That's fine, but it can't be everything. You are more than just a parent, you're a person, too," Marge points out.

I sigh. "Yeah. Sometimes it seems like there isn't room to just be me. It's been hard. Errol convinced me to come talk to you. I agreed because I—" I shake my head because I can't seem to force out the words to finish the thought. "Errol took me on a date before we got back together. He said he wanted me to have a break from being Papa. A few hours to just be Rene. Other than skating, that was my first actual break since I had Mo."

"Ice skating?"

"Hockey at McGill And I, uh, played one season in the NWHL for the Canadiennes."

"So what you're telling me is that other than your job, this date with Errol was the only substantial break you'd had in six years?"

"Yeah," I confirm with a sharp nod. I stuff my hands under my thighs to keep them still. "Errol's… he always… there is no one else I'd even consider having a kid with. He's special." My voice goes all soft and gooey when I talk about Errol.

"Did he tell you why he wanted you to make an appointment with me?" Marge glances down at her notes.

"Mo and I argued about his screen time. Mo was yelling things he didn't mean and Errol intervened. I froze up, it reminded me of something." I wring my hands together, remembering the fight.

"Something bad?" Marge prompts me to elaborate.

"Yeah. I used to fight with my mom and..." Nope, I still can't force out the words. I shake my head, helpless to form the words to tell the whole story. The truth has always come with consequences that hurt me more than staying silent. I can't say it. Silence stretches, a heavy hot weight that makes me squirm and resort to plucking at the pillow again, unable to meet Marge's kind eyes.

"We don't have to discuss that if you aren't ready. Can you tell me anything else about your childhood and your family of origin so I can understand better?"

"We moved a lot. My folks were kind of traditional. Mom stayed home and Dad worked. I got into hockey as a kid. Mom signed me up for figure skating as soon as I could balance on a skate blade, but I loved watching hockey with Dad. Watching games together was the only time he seemed to like me. As soon as I got a choice, I traded in my toe picks for pads. I was good enough to make a travel team, and later elites and a junior team. They let me keep playing as long as I kept my grades up at school."

"That must have required a lot of dedication," Marge says.

"Yeah," I nod. This is much safer ground. "Hockey was where I got to express myself. I didn't have to live up to gendered expectations on the ice. We were all just hockey players, no matter which league I played with. I mean, not that it was always easy. It crushed me the first year I had to play on a girl's team instead of it just being all of us on the ice like for peewees. Once I got on the ice, it was still the game I loved, regardless."

"And off the ice?" Marge pivots and I answer without

thinking about it.

"My mom wanted me to be more girly. She wanted a daughter she could take shopping and do spa days with. The hockey made her push it even harder. We fought a lot."

"Did it escalate beyond verbal arguments?"

"Not with Mom," I hedge and then I hold my breath because that's tantamount to admitting it escalated with Dad.

"And your father?" Marge's tone betrays no emotion, just a mild interest, and that makes it easier to admit.

"He had a drinking problem."

Silence for a beat. Marge gives me space to elaborate on that point. I don't.

"You don't have to share anything you find too difficult. However, I want to assure you that nothing you say will shock me. Or alter how I see you," Marge assures me when the silence drags on to become uncomfortable again.

"How do you see me?" I challenge her.

"I see a passionate young person who overcame a lot to stand before me with a family they care about deeply. Someone who worked hard to carve out a job they love in a field that isn't always the most accepting of LGBTQ2+ people," Marge states.

"You do?" I blink at her, surprised that she seems to see the real me.

"Sure." Marge nods and flashes me a smile.

"Okay." I take a deep breath and let it out in a long hiss. "It's hard to talk about. Every time I spoke up as a kid, it meant moving before anyone could make trouble for Dad. The last counselor I told tried to use it to keep me from being able to transition. He said I was using surgery and hormones to run away from past trauma and abuse. He didn't believe that I had memories of dysphoria way before my dad ever laid a hand on me in anger."

"I'm sorry you had that experience. It's my practice to believe my patients when they tell me who they are. You made it clear you're a masc nonbinary person. Do you think abuse shaped that identity?" Marge asks.

"No." I shake my head. This is a topic I grappled with after my ill-fated first attempt at counseling put the possibility into my head, but I know the truth. "My dad hit me because he was a mean drunk. He'd have done it regardless of what was in my pants or how I presented. He only shaped my gender identity in that I didn't feel safe telling my folks about who I was. So I didn't have many safe places to explore it as a kid. Maybe if I'd had supportive parents, I'd have been able to transition sooner. But that would have fucked up my hockey career. It's just as well I didn't have the option. Anyway. That's why I came to see you today. Because my sperm donor used to smack me around and I had a flashback with Mo and Errol. It scared my kid and upset my guy, and I don't want to let that shit leak into my family and hurt them." I smooth my hands over the soft material of the throw pillow.

"Okay. We can work with that. The good news is that processing the events that caused your trauma can help you minimize further events like what you just described. There is no magic pill or overnight cure, but if you put in the work, I think we can find ways for you to deal with your past. We can find strategies together to help you stop it from overshadowing the future you are building with Mo and Errol. Sound good?" Marge offers me an encouraging smile.

"Okay." I agree.

"We're out of time for today, but I'd like to see you again next week. Does the same time work for you?"

"Yeah. Errol can watch Mo. Does he need another visit too?"

"I don't think that's necessary. If he continues to struggle with the changes in his life, we can discuss more sessions to talk and work on techniques to ease any anxieties he has. He mentioned being excited about school with the friends he made at hockey camp. Helping him make friends among his peers should ease the transition for him. You don't need a stranger to tell you this, but if it helps, you are doing fine with him."

"Phew. Now to fix my own hot mess of a life," I joke. It falls flat. Marge gives me a compassionate smile.

"That negative self-talk right there is not helpful, Rene. I'm getting the impression there's a fair amount of it in your head, am I right?"

"You got me," I focus on the framed quote behind her again. Marge nods.

"This week, your assignment is to recognize that nasty voice in your head. Whenever they tell you that you aren't good enough or try to kick you where it hurts, you call out the lie. Tell that voice that you are doing your best."

"What if it doesn't seem like a lie?" I ask.

"You are still doing the best you can. It's enough. You are enough. Keep saying it until you believe it's the truth."

"Seems simple enough." I huff out a breath.

"Simple, but maybe not easy, hmm?" Marge gives me a knowing look.

"Yep. Well, I'll try. Thanks," I set the pillow back on the couch and stand to leave.

"Not a problem, is e-transfer okay for payment?" Marge stands too, smiling warmly at me.

"Yeah. It's the email address on my intake form." I gesture toward her papers.

"Perfect. I'll send you the invoice and book you in for next week, you'll get an email confirmation."

"I'll be here," I agree. Marge walks me out of the office and I feel a bit lighter for having spoken with her. This therapy deal isn't half bad when the person on the other side of the couch bothers listening.

CHAPTER 22

2 2

Errol

The week after our counseling session passes more calmly. Mo works on his breathing exercises when he gets frustrated at bedtime. He settles into the routine with his new school and Emil picking him up for after school care. He's been in a better mood, excited about his first sleepover with a new friend from school and hockey camp.

Game night rolls around again. Theo spends half the day bouncing off the walls in our group chat with excitement. It's nice to spend an evening with my friends.

Rene's got my car for the day in case Mo calls to get picked up early, what with his recent difficulties sleeping. Our plan is for Rene to meet up with me after our game wraps. We plan to take full advantage of our kid-free night.

Theo kicks off the game session as soon as everyone is ready. We start with our preparations for what seems to be the final showdown and then make our way into the mercenary stronghold. Theo lets us split up into two groups.

Pia, Jude, and Laura, along with her dragon companion, go in through a hidden tunnel. Pia's apprentice necromancer knows about the stronghold's layout, so she leads them. That leaves my run-of-the-mill fighter, Theo's non-player character Prince Tamsin, and Gui's ranger, Carl, to approach the main gates. I'm chafing at running such a straightforward character this campaign. I get why Theo cajoled me into it, since Jude's never played VentureQuest before. And Max was also new to our group when we started. Still, I'll be happy to retire Zelphod when we move on to our next adventure.

We consider trying to send the other group to the gates to negotiate. Jude's got a decent charisma score and Laura's bard songs can buff his efforts. But since the mercenaries are anti-dragon, we figure a few human warriors might have an easier time infiltrating the camp. Pia's character goes with the dragon contingent, since these mercenaries are the ones who trapped her in her mentor's tower.

Worst case, Carl the ranger and Zelphod the fighter should be able to stand their ground and create a distraction. That will help the others sneak in to rescue the dragon prince. Of course, nothing goes to plan.

We bluff our way through the gates and get an interview with the mercenary captain. Only to discover Maximus, the evil sorcerer played by Max, is with him. The two of them are ready to take us captive and show the great elder wyrm just how serious their threats to the dragon heir's safety are.

Gui and I try to fight, only to end up incapacitated by

a spell Max stole from the necromancer we helped a few sessions ago. I roll like shit on my will save. Gui has a will of nope to begin with, so even his seventeen isn't enough to save him from an unwanted nap. Tamsin succeeds, but gets overpowered and captured, anyway. The three of us get dragged away, bound and only semi-conscious.

Then Pia's group bursts into the stronghold through the hidden passages. They get as far as Sythern's cell undetected. Outside the cell they run into the incapacitated Zelphod, Carl, and Tamsin, who are being transported under heavy guard. The second group cannot rescue the dragon heir or do anything for Gui and my characters. It's a bit of a clusterfuck.

Theo and Max seem far too pleased with themselves. Max does some villain monologuing. Then Theo doubles down on the villain act. He uses the mercenary captain NPC to wax eloquent about the evils of dragon-kind. Detailing how he and Max are designing a spell that will 'cure' the world of the dragon scourge.

It sounds super xenocidal, but they basically want to xenomorph all the dragons into a human form and trap them that way. Sounds like their end game is erasing the fact that dragons ever existed.

When they throw us into Sythern's cell, we can see that the spell works. The dragon prince is sitting there in human form, looking utterly wretched. Credit where it's due, Theo comes up with interesting narratives for his games. That wasn't a twist I'd expected. So now, besides escaping the enemy camp, we have to get Sythern the antidote to Max's evil magic. And stop the mercenaries from dosing Jude's character and Pebbles, Laura's baby dragon companion.

That's where the session ends, but I'm more invested

in this entire business than I was going into the hostage negotiations, so I'm fine with playing Zelphod a little longer.

It's already close to ten, so we agree to stop there. The entire party locked in the mercenary leaders' jail cells, with Maximus gloating over us. It's about the time I expected to wrap up tonight. Gui, Pia, and I text our significant others about meeting up for drinks. Paz doesn't work tomorrow. He and his cousin, who seems to be sticking to her latest breakup with her on-again off-again ex, are meeting us at the bar.

Pia texts Emil and I text Rene. They're both at Pia's place with Emil and Gregor. Gregor has a morning shift at his part-time nursing home side-job, so he volunteered to stay home with Rain while Emil joins us.

Emil is having a bit of a last hurrah to distract him from the looming blood test scheduled for next week to determine if the IVF cycle succeeded. Not that he's been drinking at all, but the guy is stressing about whether all the misery of the injections, medication side effects, and invasive monitoring was worth it. Or if they're starting back at square one. If anyone needs a distracting night out, it's him.

I'm looking forward to an evening out with Rene. Not to mention having the house to ourselves all night long, I hope. It'll be the first time Rene and I have complete privacy with no chance of Mo waking up and interrupting us.

CHAPTER 23

23

Rene

Emil and I take Errol's car to meet Errol and his gaming group at a bar called The Taphouse, near their work. I'm not in much of a drinking mood, so I volunteer as our designated driver. From the teasing comments that unleashes at Errol from his friends, I realize he doesn't often get the chance to let loose. That doesn't surprise me.

Errol has always had an impulse to ensure everyone around him is alright. It's an outstanding quality to have in a co-parent and I'm sure it serves him well at work too, from what he's said about his job.

"Thought you had called lifetime dibs on DD," Theo teases Errol, slinging an arm around him.

Errol rolls his eyes, but he smiles at Theo's ribbing.

"Leave him be, nothing wrong with being responsible," Jude nudges Theo.

Theo throws Jude a jaunty mock-salute and says a

teasing, "Yes, hun. Next round's on me, what do you all want?"

"Guess I'll have the house IPA, thanks," Errol orders. Jude declines alcohol, but hops up to help Theo carry the drinks back to the table.

"Think you can remember everything, Theo?" Laura teases him.

"Oh yeah, bring it on," Theo shoots back with a gesture to imply he can take whatever she dishes out.

"I'll have a vodka cranberry," Laura says.

"I'll have what she's having, make it easy on your memory," Alice, Paz's cousin, says with a flirty wink toward Laura. Laura flashes a smile and looks away coyly. There's a spark of interest between them, though neither seems ready to act on it.

Max, Gui, and Paz all order the same beer as Errol. Theo counters by saying he's just going to grab a pitcher of whatever's on tap. Since that's the house IPA, no one objects.

Pia and Emil ask for soda, so I jump on board the soda bandwagon and Theo agrees to get a pitcher of root beer, too. At first I stick close to Emil and Errol, since I know them the best, but the group is pretty open and I relax, enjoying the outing. It's fun to go out and forget my troubles for a few hours. Bars aren't my favorite hangout most of the time. Surly drunks bring up unpleasant memories, but Errol's friends are boisterous and happy and just barely buzzed, not wasted, so I can cope.

Mo called to say goodnight just before I headed over to the bar. It sounded like he's having a good time. I'm hopeful he'll make it through the night at his new friend's place, but if not I'll be good to drive to get him.

I enjoy watching Errol joke around with his friends.

They tease him about letting loose, but he stops drinking after the second beer in as many hours. He's acting a little buzzed, and horny, if his hand on my thigh under the table is anything to go by. The others discuss taking the party to the clubs, but I'm more than ready to get to the between the sheets part of the evening with Errol.

After dinner at The Taphouse, we split up. Emil and Pia are ready to head home, so as not to disturb Gregor's sleep in the wee hours. Max asks for a ride home, too. The others pay their portion of the tab and head out to dance in a raucous throng.

Errol seems surprised Laura doesn't want a ride home with us, but I'm not. She and Alice have been exchanging meaningful glances all night long, and I'd be shocked if they didn't end up at least dancing together by the end of the night.

Max calling it an early night surprises me. He got more quiet as the night progressed and the level of inhibitions around the table lowered. Max ended up as the sole single at the table with no one to flirt with. I'd have expected him to want to find some company at the party's next stop. It didn't help his mood that Theo batted his eyes at Max teasingly. Theo seemed to notice that Max felt left out, without realizing that the playful fake flirting and teasing about helping Max find a date for Theo and Jude's wedding only made Max's mood worse.

We drop Pia and Emil off first, wishing them luck at Emil's blood test first thing Monday. Then Max gives me directions out to his place. He lives across the Lion's Gate Bridge, in North Vancouver. It's a fair bit out of our way, but Max appears so relieved at not having to deal with the night bus, I don't begrudge him the detour.

I'm sure it sucks for him, being the odd one out among

all the relationship bliss going around his friend group. Errol offers to set Max up with a friend at another studio with similar taste in video games, Max gives a non-committal answer before directing me to his rental.

The views of the night-bright city from where he lives up on the sloping base of Grouse Mountain are spectacular. Errol and Max exchange their goodbyes, Max looking melancholy. Then we go home, crossing the Ironworker's bridge to get to Burnaby rather than going back through the downtown core. We make it home just after midnight.

I'm used to being the initiator with our sex life. That's how it's always been. When we were younger, Errol was often content to help me get off and then move on to other activities like games or just cuddling.

At first, I'd fretted that he wasn't that into me, since he rarely asked for sex. That was when he told me about being demi and not all that into sex in general, though he hadn't learned the label until later. When we had sex, he was into it, but it wasn't always front of mind for him the way it was for me.

Since we've rekindled our sex life, he seems just as content to follow my lead as he ever was. I used to worry our mismatched libidos might be an issue between us. That I might ask for more than he wanted to give. We got past that, though. I learned to trust Errol will tell me when he isn't into sex, and not push him. It's a two-way street, he doesn't fuss or shame me over my needs either, just participates or excuses himself to do something else as he pleases. Tonight is not one of those times where he's not into it.

Errol kisses me breathless as soon as we get inside the house. I take a minute to get used to the taste of beer on his tongue. Errol notices my uncharacteristic reserve.

"What's wrong?" he asks, searching my face.

"Nothing," I lie by reflex, then I shake my head. I can be honest with Errol. "Want to freshen up before we resume kissing?"

Errol frowns and nods. "Sorry, yeah, didn't think about it. If it upsets you, I don't have to drink next time."

"I don't mind you drinking, Errol," I say. Well, I don't want to mind. It's easy to say not everyone who drinks a beer is going to turn into my dad. It's harder to get my brain on board with that reality when that yeasty smell on his breath sends my mind to places I'd rather not go. Errol was always my escape from those bad times.

"But you don't want to kiss me when I taste like beer?" Errol puzzles out.

"Yeah. I guess not. Sorry," I say, retreating half a step.

"I'll brush my teeth. It's fine, Rene," Errol says. He rubs his palms along my arms to reassure me, searching my gaze. He doesn't seem drunk. Mostly, Errol seems concerned. "You're sure you're okay?" he checks.

"Yeah. I'm good," I say with more conviction. Errol holds my gaze a moment longer, then kisses the back of my hand before he goes to brush his teeth. While he does that, I loiter near our bed, stripping out of my clothing with deliberate care, and folding it to kill time before piling it into the hamper.

When Errol gets back, he's lost his shirt and just has on a pair of jeans with the fly undone. He takes in my nakedness and grins.

"What?" I ask, self-conscious under his gaze.

"I enjoy looking at you," he says, closing the distance between us and taking me into his arms. "You're everything I want." He kisses me, his mouth minty fresh.

"Yeah?" I say breathily when the kiss ends. "I enjoy looking at you too, lose the pants," I demand, his regard is too heavy and I need things lighter.

"Bossy much?" Errol jokes.

"Yep, I'm a real task-master, stud." I run my thumb over his lips.

Errol nips at the pad of my finger. "How do you want to do this?" Errol asks, his hands resting gently on my hips.

"I still like PIV. If you're into that," I offer with a breezy shrug. It's not as casual an offer as I make it sound. He's the only one I've ever trusted to have that kind of sex with. The only person I knew, without a doubt, wouldn't see me differently for enjoying the parts I was born with. "The type of meta I got doesn't interfere with the originally installed parts, and penetration feels amazing on my dick." That last part was more of an educated guess, since I'd only tested it out with toys.

"Do you have condoms?"

"Yeah, I was, uh, optimistic," I admit. I turn to get them from the bottom drawer of his dresser where I've started stashing my underwear and sex toys. The box of condoms rests where I left it.

I hand one to Errol and he rolls on the latex. He kisses me. His hands roam over my body, relearning all the sensitive spots that make me moan. While he's fondling me, I cup his ass the way he likes so I can grind our dicks together. It's hard to get enough stimulation standing there, so I crowd Errol up against the bed. We break off our kissing only long enough for him to lie down. Then I climb over him, straddling his hips and getting back to the kissing and grinding.

We make out like that until Errol, breathless and panting, asks, "You still want me inside you, Rene?"

"Yeah. Fuck me," I agree, lifting so he can get his dick lined up, then sinking down onto him. It's not the same as I remember, so I take it slow at first, riding him with measured movements of my hips, ramping up as I adjust to his girth. Errol reaches for me, pulling me back down so we can kiss. The new angle cranks up the intensity. It also makes for shallower thrusts, but Errol's hitting me just right. The friction as our bodies rub together is perfect on my T-dick, a slick slide of pleasure building between us.

Errol's tongue in my mouth, his dick inside me, his arms around me. It's even better knowing that Errol returns my feelings. We wouldn't be doing this if he didn't feel our connection. I never thought I could have this perfect bliss again.

This, right here, is home and happiness and I feel complete in the bone deep knowledge of Errol's love and acceptance. The orgasm that follows those thoughts is only magnified by the thrill of Errol's body tensing under me, his dick driving in deep as it pulses with his release. I swallow his groan of pleasure, kissing him hard. I rock my hips to his rhythm to draw out both our pleasure until I can't anymore.

After, I just lay on top of him in a sated slump. Our breathing evens out, neither of us moving to separate until Errol withdraws his spent cock to deal with the condom. I roll off of him and snuggle into his side.

"Good?" Errol asks softly.

"Mhm, you're still hot stuff, stud," I agree. Then, after a pause, I add, "I love you."

"Love you too, imzadi. Good night."

It doesn't take me long to fall asleep in his arms.

CHAPTER 24

Errol

Rene grinds back against my morning wood. It's nice to wake up without a kid in our bed this morning. Mo made it through the night at his friend's place without trouble. Considering his difficulties sleeping through the night without joining us for the past few weeks, we'd worried he might call for a late night pick up. Since we didn't get a call, it appears he stuck it out just fine. I'm proud of him for overcoming his nerves.

We're supposed to pick him up in a few hours, but there's plenty of time to take advantage of our kid-free morning to get each other off again. It feels like I've got years of loving Rene to make up for. No one turns me on like they do. Rene grinds against me until my dick is hard and there's a growing wet spot on my underwear. Their dick is hard against my palm as I tug them in time to the roll of their hips. Their moans drive my lust higher and

I want to feel the hard length of their erect dick in my mouth, want to suck them and give them pleasure.

"Want to taste you," I gasp near their ear.

"Same," Rene agrees. They arch their neck around to try kissing me, but the angle is awkward. They shift around to face me, suggesting, "Sixty-nine?"

"Definitely," I agree. That sounds pretty damn perfect. Rene scrambles around to get in position, their torso is shorter than mine, so we make some adjustments to get the logistics to work. We lie side by side, bodies curled together so we can get each other's dicks in our mouths.

Despite coming just last night, I don't last very long with Rene's mouth wrapped around my cock. They have more staying power, fucking my face with abandon until they climax too. It seems like the orgasm grips their entire body, racking them with pleasure. I like the way they clench and their muscles shiver and their voice gets all shivery and strained. I like everything about Rene. Afterward, we move to lay face to face again, snuggling together dozily for a few minutes, exchanging lazy kisses.

"Love having sex with you," Rene says.

"Yeah?" I ask.

"Yeah. With you, I get why people call it making love."

"Makes sense," I say. "That's what we're doing, right?"

I don't add that it's also what we're doing when we stay up late watching Star Trek or Rene's favorite baking show together on the couch, or when we make silly pancake shapes for Mo. Or when they sing along to radio jingles on our morning commute after we drop Mo off at school. There are so many little things our love is built on. The mundane daily activities that become special by virtue of doing them together. I know Rene sees that too, it doesn't need to be said. There is something I want to say to them though.

"I made you something," I say, rolling out of bed to get the framed portrait from the spot where I stashed it.

"Yeah?" Rene props themself up on an elbow to watch me.

"Sure. Nothing huge, we just sort of fell into cohabitating and I wanted to sort of mark it? Make it official and intentional, you know?"

"Are you asking me to live with you while we're laying naked in our shared bed?" Rene pokes fun at me, their smile makes me grin too.

"I guess I am. It sounds silly when you put it like that," I complain, returning to the bed with the wrapped frame and laying it on Rene's lap. "Here."

Rene tears open the paper, and gives me an awed look when they see the portrait. It's the sketch they requested from my commission page. Only, instead of Mo alone, it's the three of us together during the game night we hosted. Pia snapped the reference photo on her phone. They sent it to me when I was still waffling on whether to pursue a relationship with Rene.

In the portrait, Mo is sitting between Rene and I, arms thrown high in victory after our team won a round of *Battle Fox*. Rene and I sit on either side of him, exchanging a look that speaks volumes about the fondness between us. Even when we were still figuring out where we stood that day, the connection had been there.

"Our family," Rene says, tracing the curve of Mo's smile with a light touch.

"Yeah. I want to hang it in our home. And I want to add more. More pictures, and more memories, every year, forever. What do you say, imzadi? And, no this isn't a marriage proposal, I remember you aren't into that." I don't blame them with the marriage between their parents, I get why it feels like a trap to them. And it's not something I need as long as Rene is willing to commit to us. I'll be happy to live together and raise our son together without the piece of paper for external validation.

"Yes," Rene agrees. "It's perfect. I want a lifetime with you, too, Errol." They pull me into a hard kiss, a little nip of their teeth at the end to punctuate it.

"Good," I say. Rene sighs and snuggles into my arms. After a moment, their muscles tense, though. Like they want to pull away.

"What's wrong?" I ask, kissing their cheek.

"It's nothing bad. Just, thinking about our family, and adding more memories, like you say."

"And?" I press.

"First off, you were right about therapy. I guess I needed to talk about things. Learn better ways of coping. It just seems like taking a step back. Going from the occasional trigger to connecting my past with all the stupid shit I do and constantly thinking about it and analyzing why I do things, you know?"

"Like what?" I ask, not following.

"I dunno. Like how I was always so dead set against getting married someday, because I saw how miserable my folks were together. Or second-guessing if I was excited to take Mo to hockey camp because I wanted to share something I love with him, or if I was trying to force him to be something he's not?"

"He wanted to go to camp," I point out.

"Okay, not the best example. But like..." Rene huffs a frustrated breath, shakes their head and blurts, "Would you want a do-over? Shit, no, that isn't how I meant to ask. It's not a do-over. More another chance to get things right? Gah, no. That's not right either."

"What are you talking about?" I pull back, trying to puzzle out what they're implying.

"Another kid." Rene gestures vaguely toward Mo's room. "I want more kids in that family portrait down the line."

"You said you weren't interested in another pregnancy," I hedge.

"Yeah. My first pregnancy sucked, but I got Mo out of it. Seeing you with him, and him doting on Rain makes me think I'd be willing to try it again, if we both want another child?"

"Rene..." I trail off, unsure how to reply. I love being Mo's dad more than I ever thought I would. I'd love to have more kids with Rene. But not at the cost of hurting them, and I know their first pregnancy came with a heaping helping of trauma.

"No, just listen. I didn't actually hate being pregnant." Rene says, correctly guessing my biggest objection to the idea. "Like the actual physical parts of it weren't too bad for me. The trappings made it awful. Glowy renditions of motherhood bombarding me every time I needed anything pregnancy related from clothing to healthcare, right? But Emil says Pia saw a midwife who respected their pronouns and didn't run around calling them mom this and mother-to-be that. I think if we had another kid, if my medical care was like that, and I had you with me to support me, I could handle it."

"That's a good start, but are you certain?" I ask, unsure if I should take this offer at face value or if it's coming from a healthy place. Which I can infer from Rene's earlier comments is something they're trying to figure out, too.

"Yeah. I guess the practice Pia used is queer friendly. They also have an OB on staff, so even if I'm not eligible for midwifery care, I could still go there. But I get it, if a baby is too overwhelming. Or whatever. I just figure, we're already locked into this co-parenting thing and Mo is getting old enough to be a big help. If it's something we want, I don't want to wait too long. I would want them to grow up together. So, what do you think?" Rene rambles to a stop and watches me expectantly.

"Where is this coming from?" I ask, running my hand along their side in a soothing caress. "I don't need another kid to be happy with our family, Rene. A new baby can't give me back the years I missed out on with you and Mo."

"Okay. No, I get that. I'm screwing this up. I'm not proposing a do-over on Mo. That would be fucked up reasoning. I'm asking because I want another kid with you. A pregnancy with a supportive partner and a health-care provider who doesn't leave me traumatized. All the baby years with someone to alternate middle of the night feedings and diaper changes with. Like that portrait you're doing for Pia. I want to see you all gooey-eyed over our baby."

"I'm gooey-eyed, as you call it, over Mo," I point out. "That isn't a reason to have a second kid."

"Okay. What about just loving being Mo's papa and loving seeing you be his daddy and wanting more of that? All of that. Building a bigger family with you."

"So, you want a second child for that kid's own sake? Not to give me and Mo something you somehow think you owe us? Because I love you, Rene, and I want no part of you doing something that will hurt you out of some misguided sense of duty."

"No. I want it for me, too. For all of us," Rene insists with the certainty that brooks no further questioning. They hug the portrait of our family to their chest. "What do you say?."

"Then I'm open to it, imzadi. I hear you about the age gap between Mo and a new baby. But I want to be sure Mo feels secure here before we throw another change at him. No matter how much he says he wants a sibling. Can we take the approach of not doing anything to prevent it and seeing what happens?" I say. I'm not anywhere near ready for the sort of aggressive tactics Pia, Emil, and Gregor had to resort to.

"That's fair. I guess it will give me a chance to do things the right way. Like, stopping hormones and taking folate and stuff." Rene gestures airily to encompass all that the suggestion entails.

"Will we need to see a specialist about your fertility?" I ask.

Rene snorts. "No. I just had a simple release done. I left the original plumbing intact, so we can do this the old-fashioned way. I checked it would be possible before the operation, just in case. I only need to stop my testosterone shots. The meta might constrict things a little? It shouldn't be enough to screw with the birthing process much. I'll talk to a midwife about whether I need to see an OB or if they'd be comfortable taking me on as a patient."

"And you still like PIV," I joke, thinking about last night.

Rene winks at me. "Yeah, I do." They lean in to kiss me. "I guess I'll put a hold on my testosterone shots and we can just see what happens for a while?"

"That works for me," I agree. After all, I saw how hard it was for Emil to get knocked up after stopping T. And Rene and I had sex for years before we got Mo. It's not like this will happen right away, even if we ditch the condoms today.

"Cool. So, we both want this?" Rene asks, expression earnest.

"Yes, we do," I agree, claiming their mouth in another gentle kiss that leads to more kissing and touching. Nothing could sound better than building my future with Rene.

Eventually, we untangle ourselves from the sheets and go to get showered and ready to pick up Mo from his new friend's place. The three of us go out to brunch after we pick Mo up, then spend the day playing games together at home.

Rene coming back into my life is like succeeding on a saving throw I never realized I'd get the chance to roll. Having them back is like breathing new life into the parts of my heart I thought were as good as dead after Rene left. We don't do anything out of the ordinary, just spend the day together as a family with our son. It's perfect in a way I never dared to hope for, and my heart is fuller than it has ever been.

CHAPTER 25

Epilogue

Errol

Over the next few months, our family falls into a comfortable rhythm. Mo is less prone to full-blown tantrums after the appointment to talk things through with Rene's therapist. Him crawling into bed with us overnight still happens every so often, but the bed wetting is all but non-existent. I can't bring myself to mind him snuggling with us too much. Rene seemed exasperated the one time he knocked on our locked door while we were fooling around.

Most nights, Mo doesn't come to our bed until closer to dawn, if at all, so he's not interrupting anything but actual sleep. I guess Mo might be a bit old to sleep with his parents, but the therapist said regression was normal. He'll outgrow it, I'm not ready for that, not yet. Rene and I let him snuggle with us.

This morning we're all sleeping in because it's Mo's

birthday weekend. My folks are coming up later today to take Mo on a shopping spree. Mo video chats with them a few times a week and we've spent several weekends driving out for brief visits. Mo seems more comfortable calling my folks Gramps and Gram than he did at our first visit. Less overwhelmed by it all.

It's not their first trip our way either, so the room I set up for Rene is getting some use as a guest room. I've got a contractor lined up to make our place more suitable for the long-term. Since my upstairs tenants decided not to renew their lease, I've got huge plans to do some remodeling of the empty apartment.

The idea is to split the current three-bedroom unit upstairs into a smaller two-bedroom. I have the relevant permits lined up, and a renovation schedule that should have the major work done before the holidays, since the job mostly consists of moving a few non-load-bearing walls and a bathroom reno. We're moving the tenants' private entrance to the rear of the unit. That way we can reclaim the front portion of the upstairs to give our family more living space. I'll need to find new tenants after the renovations, but I don't expect that to pose a problem.

The contractor I hired assures me we can reconfigure the access to the second floor from our current ground level living space easily. The plan for upstairs is to put in a master suite and another small bedroom that we hope to use as a nursery. Since the two existing bedrooms are roughly the same size, Mo is keeping his room. Our current room, with the en suite, will become a guest room now that my folks want to visit all the time.

The dining nook that I hastily converted into a room for Rene, will house my home office setup. The changes should give us the space we need to continue growing our family without entirely cutting off the income from renting the second floor unit. It worked out well that my current tenants had graduated, since I'd have hated to kick them out, but we're parting on good terms, so the timing was a win.

Rene smiles at me over Mo's head. The kid lies sprawled on his back between us, and watching him there, I can't imagine my heart being any more full than it is right now.

"Morning, imzadi," I drawl, reaching for my glasses.

"Morning. I gotta pee, again," Rene grumbles, rolling out of the bed. They rush off to the bathroom, their abrupt departure rousing Mo from his slumber. He rolls closer to me and snuggles against my chest. I pat his back.

"It's 'cause the baby's on their bladder," Mo mumbles sleepily.

"What?" I ask, a little shell-shocked at the idea it could be true. Or, well, sort of true. If Rene's pregnant, there's no way they're far enough along for the fetus to be putting pressure on their bladder. But I seem to recall Pia grumbling about pregnancy making their bladder seem like more of a sieve from the start.

It's not like we've done much to prevent a pregnancy. We only used Rene's stash of condoms that first time. It's just that after watching my friends struggle with infertility for years, it's jarring that it might happen so fast for us. It's only been a few months since Rene and I decided we might want another kid and they stopped their hormone injection. I expected it to take longer. It's weird wrapping my head around the idea. And if we *are* expecting, how the hell do I tell Emil? One thing at a time. Mo's dozy wishful thinking is hardly a definitive diagnosis.

Rene flushes and comes back to bed, I can't help scrutinizing them for any other signs. There aren't any. Of course not. They *do* have a smirky self-satisfied smile on their face, though.

"Breakfast?" Rene gives me the same pleading puppy-dog eyes Mo's got perfected.

"Yeah. Ok. What do you want?" I ask, shoving aside the blankets.

"Let's go out before your folks arrive," Rene suggests blithely.

"That sounds good. Let me grab a quick shower," I shuffle toward the bathroom.

"You do that, stud." Rene winks at me. "I'll get Momo ready."

I blink off the sense of weirdness. Mo is just putting ideas in my head. I go into the bathroom and take a quick shower before dressing.

When I go out into the living room, Rene has Mo dressed and ready to leave. Something is off about their wide smile. Rene is bubbling with contained excitement that I'm sure has nothing to do with my parents visiting, although they are getting along again. And Mo's shirt is new.

It's an Ollie Owl design, but not the one my friends got printed special for him. This one has Red, the fox character from the game, standing next to Ollie. I read the caption. Ollie has the label, 'big brother', Red's label reads, 'player 2 is joining the game.'

I glance between Mo and Rene.

"For real?" I ask, still processing.

Rene nods. "For real." They look uncertain now, like they don't know if I'm happy with the news. That won't do at all. I sweep them into a hug, kissing them deep enough to make Mo groan over his parents' PDA. Guess I need to get on those renovations ASAP.

"What?" Mo asks.

"Read your shirt, buddy," Rene suggests. Mo stretches the shirt out away from his body to read the caption.

"Big brother? Really? You're getting me a baby sibling?" He asks, bouncing on his toes.

"We are, as long as everything with the pregnancy is healthy," Rene says cautiously.

"Yes!" Mo latches on to Rene, hugging them tight. "Best birthday ever!"

Rene picks the kid up and kisses his cheeks. Mo giggles. I bite my tongue against telling Rene to take it easy. Pia just about beat it into my head that treating pregnant people like they're made of glass is BS. They definitely drummed home the point that if it's something they'd have done before pregnancy they can still do it now, barring complications.

"How long have you known?" I ask instead of fussing. Only realizing after the words leave my mouth that Rene might take them as a reminder of our history. They flinch and I reach for them, wanting to reassure them I'm not accusing them of anything.

"Only since yesterday. I wasn't hiding it or anything. Felt off after my morning coffee, so I picked up a test. Got the shirt made on my lunch break," Rene gives me a worried look. "I wanted it to be special. Are you mad?"

I kiss them again, taking Mo and settling him on my hip, my other hand splayed over Rene's belly, as if there's anything to feel there at this early stage. "No. I'm excited. This is what we wanted, right?" Now I'm the worried one. Worried they might have changed their mind about wanting this.

"It is. I'm excited, too. We have our first appointment in about eight weeks."

"Do we?" I ask, surprised.

"Yeah, I might've called the midwife Pia recommended as soon as I saw the second line on the test. It was super weird looking at it and wanting it to be positive this time."

"Can I name the new baby?" Mo asks.

"You can help us think of names, but Daddy gets the final say, since I got to name you, Momo," Rene says.

"You're the one carrying the kid, what do you want to call this one?" I ask.

"For now? Blueberry pancake or maybe bacon. Or waffles, because I'm freaking starving. I forgot how ravenous making a tiny human makes me," Rene jokes.

That makes Mo and I laugh. I set Mo on his feet and steer him toward the door. "We better get a move on then. Time to feed the pregnant papa before he loses patience and gobbles us right up," I tickle Mo and he giggles.

We leave the house to celebrate the news and Mo's birthday. We've got so much to celebrate, and I can't wait to spend the rest of my life loving Rene and the family we're building together.

Thanks for reading Saving Throw! If you enjoyed it, be sure to leave a review. The Table Topped series continues with Plus One Bonus, Max's story. Make sure you've got the whole series, available at: https://www.amzn.com/B08R6LM6YG

And for weekly snippets from upcoming releases, check out my FB group at: https://www.facebook.com/

groups/alexsalcove

Glossary of French Terms

Chapter 2	
Quand nous arrivons	When we arrive
Pourquoi donc?	Why?/Why is that?
Pas fait dodo	Not napping
notre voiture?	our car
Ça me manque	I miss it (the car)
Papa est grincheux	Papa is grumpy
Désolé, Papa	Sorry, Papa
Il t'aimera fort comme le ciel, mon chou	He'll love you like the sky, baby
Ouais?	Yeah?
aussi	too
mon petit chou	baby (literally my little cabbage)
Chapter 3	
Salut, Papa dit que...	Hi, Papa said that...
Seulement un peu d'école, mon chou	Only a little from school, my dear
mon petit monstre	my little monster
Chapter 7	
Bien sûr, mon chou	Of course, my dear
Tu vas bien?	You doing okay?
ouais	yeah
Je dis prems	I call dibs
Jouer avec nous, Papa!	Play with us, Papa!

Jouons!	let's play
Chapter 10	
J'ai faim	I'm hungry
Nous pouvons acheter des sandwiches	We can buy sandwiches
Est-ce une promesse?	Do you promise?

ABOUT THE AUTHOR

Alex Silver (he/him) grew up mostly in Northern Maine and is now living in Canada with one spouse, two kids, and three birds. Alex is a trans guy who started writing fiction as a child and never stopped. Although there were detours through assisting on a farm and being a pharmacist along the way.

Visit me online at:

http://alexsilverauthor.wordpress.com/

Join my Facebook group at:

https://www.facebook.com/groups/alexsalcove

Follow me on BookBub at:

https://www.bookbub.com/profile/alex-silver

Sign up for my newsletter for a free short story at: https://landing.mailerlite.com/webforms/landing/i2w6l7

And as always, consider leaving a review on Amazon or Goodreads if you enjoyed this book, reviews are of vital importance to independent authors, thanks!

TABLE TOPPED

Roll for Initiative Book 1 January 2021 www.amzn.com/B08R6M1XBT
Charisma Check Book 2 January 2021 www.amzn.com/B08R6J14VZ
Saving Throw Book 3 February 2021 www.amzn.com/B08SL3WF2Q
Plus One Bonus Book 4 Coming Soon

Charisma Check

Gui's the best friend I ever had. I love him like a brother, too bad I'm falling for *his* little brother.

Jude is a walking talking temptation, everything I never let myself want. He's sweet as chocolate, wickedly funny, and he gets me. The sex, well, it's worth a repeat and that's something I never do.

When he visited Gui, I thought I could settle for a one night stand, but then Jude moves to my city to work at my studio. Gui gets him to join my gaming group and suddenly he's all I see. Now Jude's looking at me with hearts in his eyes and I'm terrified that I'm going to break his heart.

Charisma Check is the second M/M romance in the Table Topped series. It features Jude, a hopeless romantic with diabetes who makes animation and Theo, a commitment-phobic trans man with depression who runs tabletop games for his friends. www.amzn.com/B08R6J14VZ

CW: for severe depression, gender dysphoria, mention of past suicidality, surgical recovery, injection medications/needles (insulin dependent diabetes)

Saving Throw

Rene was my first everything. Best friend, first kiss, first love, first heartbreak.

Seven years after walking out of my life, they tear open old wounds with a single photo of a smiling little boy and the message they're coming home.

Mo has my smile and Rene's eyes. It kills me that I didn't know about him sooner. As furious as the news Rene kept such a major secret makes me, I want a relationship with my son more than I want to rehash old arguments. Besides, Rene has more baggage than the 747 they flew in on, and I swore off love the first time they left me heartbroken.

When I learn Rene and Mo need a place to stay while they settle into life in Vancouver, it sounds like a perfect opportunity. I've got a spare room. What better way to figure out co-parenting than living together? It's not like I'm going to fall for the ex who hurt me deeper than anyone else could. That would be ridiculous.

Saving Throw is the third M/NB romance in the Table Topped series. It features Errol, demisexual panromantic production coordinator who likes to be in control and his first love, Rene, a non-binary trans masc ex-hockey player turned coach.

CW: Past mentions of a physically abusive alcoholic parent and portrayals of trauma/PTSD related to that, secret teenage pregnancy and related gender dysphoria/difficulty with accessing medical care. Side characters struggle with infertility.

HAUNTASTIC HAUNTS SERIES

Dan's Hauntastic Haunts Investigates: Goodman Dairy (*Book 1*)

Dan's Hauntastic Haunts Investigates: Hawk Lake (*Book 2*)

Dan's Hauntastic Haunts Investigates: Ivarsson School (*Book 3*)

Drew's Haunted Hangout (*A Hauntastic Haunts Short Story 1*)

Rafael's Haunted Halloween (*A Hauntastic Haunts Short Story 2*)

Lee's Haunted Holiday (*A Hauntastic Haunts Short Story 3*)

Drew's Haunted Hangout

What if your imaginary boyfriend wasn't so imaginary?

Drew was no stranger to feeling ostracized from his peers. His obsession with the paranormal began young. When he befriended Toby, the dead boy who lives in his garage.

Drew was the weird unathletic kid everyone avoided on the playground. As a teen, he found understanding in an online community created by a paranormal investigations vlogger.

Falling in love with Toby only made Drew's interest in ghosts more intense. But when he discovered Toby's striking resemblance to an unresolved missing person report, he didn't know how to help his ghost boyfriend.

At a loss, Drew turned to his online idol for help. The truth could set Drew and Toby both free, or destroy everything between them.

This is a young adult paranormal MM short story. http://eepurl.com/dNcScQ

Dan's Hauntastic Haunts Investigates: Goodman Dairy

When ghosts reach across the veil, Daniel Collins is there to tell their stories.

Dan is a vlogging ghost hunter. He has devoted his life to documenting paranormal activity. In his converted van, he travels around the country exploring haunted sites. He loves the thrill of filming restless spirits.

Chad Brewer, skeptic, works for an insurance company. He doesn't believe in ghosts, but watching Dan's vlog is his guilty pleasure. The cute vlogger is accident prone. He has Chad's work extension on speed-dial. The two talk whenever Dan gets hurt during an investigation, a frequent occurrence.

When Chad loses his job for approving too many claims, Dan offers him a position as his personal assistant. The pair sets out to investigate a haunted dairy barn for the vlog's next video series. The catch is that they must live and work together in Dan's tiny traveling home.

As the paranormal activity at the haunted dairy ramps up, so does the romantic tension between the two men. Can the love between a skeptic and a social media sensation conquer a vengeful ghost?

Dan's Hauntastic Haunts is a paranormal MM romance between a gay vlogger and his trans personal assistant. Buckle up for a hauntastic good time.

www.amzn.com/B07YSV2ZNQ

PSIONS OF SPIRE SERIES

Shelter	Novella 0.5	February 2019
Bright Spark	Book 1	February 2019
Bold Move	Novella 1.5	February 2019
Keen Sense	Book 2	April 2019
Weak Link	Novella 2.5	June 2019
Quick Fire	Book 3	July 2019
Clear Sight	Book 4	March 2020

New Ground A SPIREverse daddy kink standalone November 2020

***

Links:

Shelter www.amzn.com/B07NM9XL8K
Bright Spark www.amzn.com/B07NZ8KPS6
Bold Move www.amzn.com/B07YVGZXDM

Keen Sense	www.amzn.com/B07R6L8W91
Weak Link	www.amzn.com/B07T4J2LJZ
Quick Fire	www.amzn.com/B07VGTF3NB
Clear Sight	www.amzn.com/B07ZQP7BDS
New Ground	www.amzn.com/B08NHQFJDZ

Shelter

Family is what you make it.

Former foster kid and abuse survivor, Elliott Sheffield, lost everything when he developed telepathy at twelve years old. He's used to not relying on anyone. There are worse things than being lonely and alone, even for a psion who craves closeness. He has plans for his life and nothing can distract him from proving that he can succeed. That will show everyone who cast him aside. Especially his former best friend Caleb Gaetz.

Pansexual, poly, psion, Caleb is comfortable with all of those labels. Life seems easy for Caleb. He has a supportive family and a vibrant social life. The future will figure itself out. For the present he plans to enjoy his university years to the fullest extent possible. He knows his hedonistic tendencies irritate his former best friend, Elliott, to no end. He just doesn't understand why Elliott takes Caleb's sex life so personally.

When life throws them both curve balls, they must adjust their visions for the future to one that will give them both a happily ever after, or risk their plans falling apart.

This urban fantasy romance contains an open M/M relationship, mention of past abuse, and positive HIV status. www.amzn.com/B07NM9XL8K

Bright Spark

Sometimes growing up means giving up your preconceptions.

Aaron Anderson and Jake Moretti were childhood sweethearts until Aaron developed psionic abilities that turned both of their worlds upside down and tore them apart.

Six years later they reconnect when Aaron returns home to work with a youth summer camp affiliated with SPIRE. Jake is at the same camp, along with his current partners, to protest the organization funding it. Sparks fly when the couple reunites and Aaron discovers hidden abilities that bring him to the attention of SPIRE.

Aaron and Jake have every intention of seizing their second chance at love. But once more, forces outside their control are at play. And the organization Aaron believes in is at the center of events targeting vulnerable youth.

This urban fantasy romance contains M/M and an open M/M/M relationship. www.amzn.com/B07NZ8KPS6

www.ingramcontent.com/pod-product-compliance
Lightning Source LLC
LaVergne TN
LVHW091052080826
845145LV00002B/714

* 9 7 8 1 7 7 7 3 5 6 3 7 8 *